CODE ForeveR

ATHANASIOS VOULGARIS

Published by ATHANASIOS VOULGARIS, 2024.

"CODE F _ _ _ _ _ R"

For my wife, Effie,

my companion at every step,

my inspiration along the paths I tread, and my light at the end of each journey.

With all my love.

Summary

A man loses his beloved in a tragic accident, plunging him into despair. But as fragments of the past begin to come together, he realizes her death might not have been as accidental as he once believed. In his quest for the truth, he encounters a mysterious woman named Myrto, who claims to have her own unsettled scores with the same "enemies."

Bound by their thirst for revenge and a fierce desire to solve the mystery, the two develop an intense romance that draws them deeper into a world of dark secrets, betrayals, and relentless dangers. As their investigation unravels, they discover a code that Daphne had entrusted to Aris without his knowing—a code that could reveal critical information about their adversaries.

With each step, they uncover a more ruthless world than they ever imagined. And when the truth finally comes to light, it exposes a betrayal that leaves an indelible mark, forcing the heroes—and the reader—to question the value of revenge and the cost that truth demands.

A story brimming with passion, suspense, and unexpected twists that will keep you on the edge of your seat until the very last page.

The Clue That Changed Everything

Night had fallen heavily over the city, casting dark shadows over the buildings and streets. Aris walked slowly, lost in thought, holding a small, worn journal in his hand—Daphne's journal. It was the first time he'd dared to open it since her death. Until now, it had felt too painful, like reopening wounds that might never heal.

As he flipped through its pages, a faint line scrawled in pencil caught his eye. It read:

"Everything feels wrong, as if something lurks in the shadows. If anything happens to me, it's no accident."

Her words were both clear and cryptic. What was she afraid of? Why had she never spoken to him about her fears? His heart pounded faster, a surge of anger rising within him. Daphne wasn't careless; she wouldn't have done anything dangerous without reason. What could have happened?

As Aris continued walking, he found himself at the last place Daphne had been seen—a small café at the edge of the city. It had begun to rain lightly, and the few patrons in the café cast curious glances at the stranger standing in the corner, looking around as though searching for something only he could understand.

Suddenly, a faint scent of jasmine reached his nose. He turned and saw a woman with dark, enigmatic eyes watching him. Her gaze was filled with sorrow, yet something else lingered—a knowing look, as if she held secrets. She approached him slowly, studying him, as though trying to read his thoughts.

"Are you looking for something... or someone?" she asked, her calm voice tinged with a hidden darkness.

Aris remained silent for a moment. Something about her presence made him feel uneasy, yet strangely connected to her. "Daphne... do you know something about Daphne?" he asked hesitantly.

The woman gave a faint smile. "I knew her. Perhaps better than you think." He frowned, but her gaze held him—magnetic and intense. "I'm not here to deceive you, Aris," she added, her voice challenging. "I came to give you something, if you can bear to see beyond the obvious."

Myrto handed him a small envelope, sealed with a strange symbol he had never seen before. "Inside is the beginning of the story... or the end, depending on what you're looking to find. But I warn you, things are not as they seem."

Aris felt his mind clouded with questions and emotions. He was certain that the envelope was somehow tied to Daphne. He opened it and found a small piece of paper with only an address—a location unfamiliar to him. As he turned back to look at Myrto for an explanation, she had vanished into the rain, leaving him alone, overwhelmed by the mysteries she had revealed.

Aris gripped the envelope tightly and took a deep breath. He knew, from the look in Myrto's eyes, that he was about to step onto a dangerous path—he could feel it in his gut.

The Beginning of the Quest

The rain had intensified, and the streets were nearly deserted, much like Aris's scattered thoughts, mingling with the sound of raindrops and the faint city lights. The address on the paper led him to an old, abandoned building in the suburbs. Its walls were crumbling, and the sign at the front was worn by time, barely legible, hinting that it had once been a small warehouse.

Aris moved forward slowly, each step filling him with doubt, yet his curiosity about Myrto and the clues she had left behind overpowered any hesitation. There was something enigmatic about this woman—a dark allure that, without him realizing it, was drawing him into places he'd never imagined he'd find himself.

When he entered, darkness engulfed him. A cold draft swept through the space, and the smell of mold and neglect choked the air. He ventured further, and as his eyes adjusted to the dim light, he noticed something unusual on the wall—a series of photographs taped up, each one featuring Daphne. Daphne laughing, walking, looking over her shoulder, as if sensing someone following her.

Among the photos, one had a red circle drawn around the face of a man standing in the shadows, deep in the background. Aris felt his heart clench. He didn't recognize the face, but the presence of this unknown man stirred a sense of unease. "Who was he? An enemy or someone trying to protect her?" he wondered.

Just as he was about to pick up one of the photos, he heard a noise behind him. He spun around and saw Myrto standing at the entrance, her gaze steady on him.

"I couldn't leave you here alone," she said, her voice carrying a familiarity that took him by surprise. "Much of what you're seeing isn't coincidental. Just like your being here isn't a coincidence."

Aris looked at her with suspicion. "Why are you following me? And how do you know so much about Daphne?"

Myrto stepped forward slowly, stopping in front of him, her eyes filled with intensity. "Daphne and I shared the same enemies, Aris. I wanted answers too, and that man in the photos..." She paused, choosing her words carefully. "He was someone she once trusted, but the game changed."

Aris raised an eyebrow. "And who says I want to play your game?"

Myrto's smile was thin, laced with bitterness and tension. "You don't have a choice. Daphne wasn't just a victim. She was part of something far bigger than you could ever imagine."

Her words ignited Aris's anger. He felt as though he was trapped in a web he couldn't escape. Clenching his teeth, he asked, his voice filled with frustration, "What do you gain from this? What are you hiding?"

Myrto looked at him calmly. "I'm hiding things that will come to light when the time is right. You have to decide whether you'll stay in your pain or seek the truth. Everything else, Aris, is just details."

Her words echoed in his mind as Aris clenched his fists, a surge of revenge overtaking him. Myrto placed a small piece of paper on the table—a new address. "If you want to continue, meet me here tomorrow. If not, you'll live with your doubts forever."

Aris stood in silence as she walked away, leaving him alone in the dark. He knew the choice was his, but he also knew he couldn't stop.

The Game Begins

The night passed slowly, with Aris reflecting on Myrto's words and the weight of Daphne's photos lingering in his mind. Dawn found him exhausted, yet determined to follow the next lead—the address Myrto had given him.

The location was in a remote area near old warehouses. As he approached, he noticed that the building was different from the last one. Here, the walls were clean, freshly painted, and showed no signs of neglect. The setting seemed almost threatening in its precision, as if someone had prepared it, expecting him.

Entering, he found himself in a large room resembling a conference hall, with chairs arranged in a circle. In the center was a large table, and on it lay an envelope with his name on it. Aris eyed it suspiciously before opening it. Inside, he found a detailed report on Daphne's life, filled with dates and events he had never known.

Suddenly, footsteps echoed behind him, and he turned abruptly, bracing himself for the worst. Myrto reappeared, this time accompanied by a man with a stern expression and a cold demeanor.

"This is Michalis," Myrto said firmly. "He's helping us piece together the puzzle."

Michalis examined him closely, his gaze weighing and assessing Aris's resilience. "Aris, you have no idea how deep this story runs. Daphne wasn't merely a victim—she was a pawn in a game that goes beyond our lives. She was entangled in matters connected to people who prefer to stay hidden."

Aris felt his blood run cold. "Why didn't she tell me? Why didn't she show me what she was going through?"

Myrto gently touched his shoulder, sadness in her gaze. "Maybe she was trying to protect you. But now, there's no turning back."

Before Aris could react, Michalis stepped closer and handed him yet another envelope. "Inside is a list of people connected to Daphne's case. Some may be innocent, others not. But each of them has played a part, however small, in the truth you're seeking."

Aris looked at the envelope with a mixture of anticipation and dread. He knew that once he opened it, there would be no going back. He would be drawn into a dark path where no one could protect him, and where the boundaries between truth and lies would blur.

With his hand trembling slightly, he opened the envelope. The first page held the name of a stranger, but the second revealed something he hadn't expected. Among the names was someone he knew—a friend he'd trusted, someone he'd never imagined could be involved.

The shock was so intense that, for a moment, he felt his heart stop. He looked at Myrto and Michalis, trying to mask the pain and turmoil inside him. Something in Myrto's expression showed she understood exactly what he was going through.

"This is just the beginning, Aris," Myrto told him. "If you want to continue, you must be prepared for the worst. No one is innocent in this game. Not even you."

The truth of Aris's journey was only just unfolding, and every step he took from here on would bring him closer to a revelation that would change everything.

The First Clue

The rain had stopped, but the dampness in the air still weighed heavily. Aris walked through the city streets, lost in thought, gripping the envelope tightly. The presence of his friend's name on that list had shaken him. Nikos, who had been there for him countless times and stood by him through his darkest moments—could he really be entangled in something so sinister?

His steps led him directly to Nikos's house. Without hesitation, he rang the doorbell. A moment later, Nikos opened the door, his smile fading quickly when he saw the intensity on Aris's face.

"Aris, what's going on?" he asked, concern evident in his voice.

Aris struggled to keep his composure. "We need to talk, Nikos. It's serious."

Nikos nodded, stepping aside to let him in. As they sat in the living room, Aris scrutinized his friend, searching for any trace of lies or secrets in his expression. "Nikos, do you know what this list means?" he said, pulling the paper from the envelope and showing him his name.

Nikos froze for a moment, his expression unreadable, perhaps even shocked. He leaned forward, reading the names. When he looked back up, his eyes held a mixture of surprise and fear.

"Aris... this... I don't know what this is," he whispered, struggling to find his words. "Who gave this to you?"

"A woman who claims to know what really happened to Daphne. Her name is Myrto, and she talks about people with connections to dark interests. And your name, Nikos, is on that list. Tell me, what do you know?"

Nikos stared at the floor, as if trying to recall something he'd tried hard to bury. Eventually, he stood up and walked to the window, gazing outside with a heavy look.

"Aris, there's something I need to tell you that I've never shared with anyone. A few years ago, I got mixed up, unintentionally, with some people who... who were involved in things that were questionable, dark. It was the worst decision of my life, and by the time I realized how serious it was, it was too late to escape. I tried to distance myself, but the consequences were more severe than I could have imagined."

Aris felt every nerve in his body tense. He had known Nikos had a troubled past, but he hadn't imagined it could be connected to Daphne's tragic story.

"And what does this have to do with Daphne? Was she involved in any of it?"

Nikos hesitated, the weight of his silence almost unbearable. Finally, he turned to face Aris, his eyes filled with regret. "I don't know if she was directly involved, but I do know that some of the people I was tangled up with... they knew about her. I overheard things, conversations that mentioned her name. At the time, I didn't think much of it—I thought it was just talk. But now... now I think there's more to it."

Aris's heart sank as his worst fears began to take shape. He clenched his jaw, feeling a mix of anger and despair. "Why didn't you tell me any of this before?"

Nikos's voice broke slightly as he replied, "I wanted to protect you, Aris. I thought if I stayed quiet, if I kept my distance from those people, nothing would happen. I never imagined it would end like this."

Silence filled the room, the weight of unspoken truths hanging heavily between them. Aris looked at his friend, torn between anger and understanding. The betrayal felt raw, but he could see the remorse in Nikos's eyes—remorse that told him that, despite everything, Nikos hadn't wanted any of this.

Myrto's words echoed in his mind: *"No one is innocent in this game. Not even you."*

Nikos turned slowly to face him, his voice filled with guilt. "I don't know, Aris. But someone among those people started asking about her. I didn't understand why, but for some reason, Daphne had caught their attention. I tried to protect her, but they wouldn't let me get too close. They warned me to stay away."

Aris felt the truth choking him, like thorns in his throat. Daphne had been living with a secret, a fear she hadn't shared with him. And Nikos, his friend, might have unknowingly opened the door to these dangerous people.

"Nikos, if you've done something that cost her life, I'll find out," he said coldly.

Nikos looked at him with pain and sorrow. "I never wanted to hurt her, Aris. But some people don't forgive, and they don't forget."

At that moment, Aris's phone buzzed with a message from an unknown number:

"If you keep going, you'll pay the price she did."

Aris showed Nikos the message. "Who's playing this game, Nikos? Who's behind all of this?"

Nikos closed his eyes, as if afraid of the answer that would come, and whispered, "It's not just one person... Aris. It's an entire organization. And we've just stepped into their web."

Into the Spider's Web

The message Aris had received wouldn't leave his mind. The threats were clear, and his intuition now warned him that what he was chasing wasn't just a random truth—it was a dark secret, buried deep within the web of a dangerous organization.

After his meeting with Nikos, he felt the need to step back and think through his next move. However, before he could decide, he received another message. This time it was from Myrto:

"If you're ready to face the truth, come to the old factory on Acheloos Street tonight at ten. The doors you open won't close easily."

Aris took one last look at the message, feeling an unsettling mix of fear and curiosity. He knew that whatever awaited him at the old factory would be crucial to his investigation—perhaps his chance to uncover the real truth behind what had happened to Daphne.

That night, at a quarter to ten, he found himself in front of the abandoned factory. The place was dark and deserted, with broken windows hinting at its forgotten past. The walls were covered in graffiti and dampness, and the atmosphere felt cold and heavy.

As soon as he stepped inside, Aris followed a corridor that led to a large room filled with chairs and desks, as if it had once been a meeting space. In the distance, a figure stood silently by the window, gazing out. It was Myrto.

"I was expecting you to come," she said without turning around.

Aris approached cautiously. "You sent me the message, and here I am. I'm ready to learn whatever it takes. I want to know everything, no matter the cost."

Myrto turned slowly to face him, her expression serious. "Daphne uncovered things she was never supposed to find. Information that threatened people who are both powerful and dangerous. She was caught in this web long before you met her, and when they realized she had discovered their secrets, it was already too late."

Her voice trembled slightly, but her resolve was unmistakable. "There's a system, a hidden organization pulling strings throughout the city. They control business deals, political interests, and every kind of dark affair. Daphne tried to gather evidence, but she was betrayed."

Aris clenched his fists, his anger rising for the fate of the woman he loved. "And who betrayed her? Was it someone close to her... someone close to us?"

Myrto stepped closer and gently placed her hand on his shoulder. "There's someone within your circle who knew more than you realize. It's hard to accept, but the friend you trusted may not be as innocent as you thought."

"Nikos..." Aris whispered, and suddenly his mind filled with doubt and fear. He didn't know if he could trust anyone anymore—not even himself.

Before he could fully process this revelation, the sound of heavy footsteps shattered the silence. Myrto glanced toward the door, and a look of concern crossed her face. "We're not alone," she whispered. "Someone's following us."

Aris grabbed her hand, and together they moved quickly toward the factory's back exit. The footsteps grew louder behind them, and shadows cast along the walls hinted at others in pursuit.

As they reached the back exit, they slipped into the dark of the night, running toward the small wooded area that stretched behind the factory. Their pursuers were close, and their anxiety mounted. Each step, each breath brought them closer to the truth—but also closer to the lurking danger.

Finally, after running for what felt like an eternity, they found refuge in a small cabin at the edge of the forest. Through the trees, they could see the silhouettes of their pursuers scarching, but the shadows of the night kept them hidden.

Myrto looked at him with a gaze full of determination. "From here on, Aris, we're on our own. If you want to continue, you need to be prepared to face everything."

Driven by anger and resolve, Aris nodded. "I won't stop, Myrto. Whatever I have to sacrifice, I will find out what happened to her."

Myrto tightened her grip on his hand. "Then we're ready. But remember: the truth is never simple. And our enemies won't stop until they've erased us from the map."

Their journey was just beginning.

Hidden Paths

The night was heavy, the dark branches of the trees blocking out the stars, making the atmosphere feel almost suffocating. The cabin where they had found shelter was small, dusty, and filled with cobwebs. Myrto sat quietly in a corner, while Aris leaned against the wall, lost in thought about everything that had unfolded. Danger lingered in the air, but his determination hadn't wavered.

"Myrto, I need to know. Are you with me, or are you part of this game?" he asked, his gaze piercing her with suspicion and doubt.

Myrto looked at him calmly, almost sadly. "If I weren't with you, I wouldn't be here, Aris. The risks I've taken to get this far are immense. I have my own losses, my own unfinished business. You're not the only one who's hurting."

The tension eased slightly, and for the first time, Aris felt he might be able to trust her. "Then tell me. What's the next step?"

Myrto pulled out an old map from her coat. "There's a place in the city where the powerful meet in secret, away from prying eyes. It's an underground building, worn and abandoned on the outside, but inside it hides another reality. This is where those who lurk in the shadows gather to plan their next moves."

Aris studied the map, noting the marked location she described. He recognized it—it was a place he had passed by many times but had never imagined held something so dangerous within.

"How do we get in?" he asked, trying to visualize their next move.

Myrto looked up, a spark of daring in her eyes. "Tomorrow night, there's a meeting there. I know someone who can get us inside without drawing attention. But we'll have to be careful. One wrong move, and we won't make it out alive."

Aris felt his heart tighten, but his mind was set. If this meeting could give him answers, he was ready to take the risk.

The next night, dressed inconspicuously in plain clothes with their faces partially covered, they found themselves outside the old building. The darkness provided the perfect cover, and the city seemed to have fallen into an eerie slumber. The contact Myrto had arranged was waiting at the entrance—a young man in a wide-brimmed hat, with a mysterious look in his eyes. He motioned silently for them to follow.

The three of them slipped through a narrow side door, which led to a dark, narrow staircase descending deep underground. The light was minimal, and each step echoed as if peeling away layers of the dark secrets hidden below.

Once they reached the underground space, Aris and Myrto stopped behind a concealed corner, watching intently. The hall in front of them was filled with well-dressed individuals engaged in hushed conversations. At the center of the room was a table covered in documents and plans, while some men pointed to maps and notes, their discussions intense.

"These are the city's power players, Daphne's real enemies," Myrto whispered, gripping Aris's hand to steady him. "The truth is right in front of us."

Aris felt his anger rising but knew he had to stay calm. One careless move could ruin everything. As he strained to catch the conversations, Aris heard someone mention Daphne's name.

"We need to stay silent and listen," Myrto whispered. "This is our only chance to learn the truth."

The man speaking was someone of prominence, with an authoritative tone and a cold stare. "Daphne made the mistake of uncovering things she shouldn't have. We had to stop her. It was the only way to protect our organization."

Aris froze. His worst fear had just been confirmed. These people had orchestrated Daphne's murder to protect their secrets. Rage surged within him, and he took a step forward, but Myrto held him back.

"Don't do it, Aris. This isn't the moment," she whispered firmly. "We need evidence, and we have to get out of here alive."

He looked at her, the inner conflict tearing him apart. He wanted to shout, to expose them all, but he knew she was right. His fury would have to wait, at least for now.

Myrto pulled him gently, and the two began to retreat silently toward the exit. Their hearts pounded, but the fear of being discovered was even stronger. They knew that if they were found, they wouldn't make it out alive.

Once they made it back to the street, they finally breathed a sigh of relief. But Aris knew there was no turning back now. He had seen the faces of the people responsible for Daphne's death and had heard their confession with his own ears. This truth was a heavy burden, but it was also his fuel to keep going.

"This is just the beginning, Myrto," he said with conviction. "We'll expose them all, one by one. Daphne will have justice."

Myrto nodded, her gaze filled with unspoken promises and a bitter resolve. "And I'll be by your side, Aris. Until the end."

Their quest for vengeance had only just begun, and the path ahead was filled with dangers and truths waiting to be uncovered.

The Web Begins to Unravel

The next morning, Aris woke with a heavy feeling. The night at the factory had brought him closer to the truth—and to danger. His mind replayed the words of that man, the cold voice that had decided to "stop" Daphne to protect their organization.

Myrto entered the room, holding two mugs of coffee and wearing a serious expression. "I know last night was hard for you, but we need to move quickly. These people won't stop if they realize we're closing in on them."

Aris looked at her and nodded. "You're right. But where do we focus? We have some clues, but we need more proof. We need something that connects each of them to Daphne's murder."

Myrto pulled a folder from her bag, packed with documents, notes, and photos. "These will help. Names, meeting places, financial records. This organization has deep roots, funded by people with serious influence."

Among the photos, Aris recognized faces from the previous night's meeting—the same man who had spoken about Daphne, along with others who seemed to hold central roles in the organization.

"One of them has ties to the city's businesses," Myrto said, pointing to a man in a sharp suit with a hardened gaze. "Dimitris Karras. If we could learn more about him and his network, we might find the evidence we need."

Aris thought intensely, analyzing every detail. "Karras... I've heard of him. He owns some of the biggest stores in the city, but he's also known for his 'shadow' dealings. If we're lucky, he might be the thread that leads us to the truth."

"But that means we'll need more support," Myrto added. "We can't just go and confront him without any preparation. We'll need someone who knows his network from the inside."

At that moment, Myrto's phone rang. The name on the screen made her pause; but after a few seconds, she answered. "Yes? All right, we'll be there. Thank you."

She ended the call and looked at Aris with determination. "It was someone who works for Karras. Word is, he's got some 'issues' with the organization. He wants to meet us tonight and share information about Karras."

Aris felt a spark of hope ignite within him. "This is the first step. If we can convince him to help us, we might find the evidence we need to bring down Karras and the rest of the organization."

That same night, they found themselves in an abandoned building near the docks, where their contact awaited—a man with a rugged look and a wary gaze. "Are you sure you want to go up against these people?" he asked, eyeing them suspiciously.

Aris stepped forward. "I have nothing left to lose. They killed the woman I loved, and I'll do whatever it takes to bring them down."

The man smirked slightly, as if he respected Aris's determination. "All right, then. I'll tell you what I know. Karras has a close circle of trusted people. They guard his secrets and manage the illegal funds. If you want to hurt him, you'll need to find his financial records. He keeps them in a hidden space in his office."

Myrto leaned in closer. "And how can we get access?"

"There's only one night when the building is completely empty. Every Sunday, when the organization has its monthly meetings out of town. If you can get in and find the records, you'll have everything you need to incriminate him."

Aris and Myrto exchanged a determined look. They knew the risk was high, but this was their only chance to gather the evidence they needed.

"We'll be there on Sunday," Aris said, looking at the man with gratitude. "And if everything goes as planned, this organization won't survive."

The man gave them one last look. "Be careful. These people don't forgive. If you expose them, you'll be their next targets."

As the man walked away, Aris and Myrto stood in silence, looking at each other. They knew that this coming Sunday would be decisive—either they would secure the proof they needed, or they would become the next targets of an unforgiving organization.

Sunday night was approaching, and the tension was building. Aris was preparing himself for the moment he would confront Karras's web, ready to expose the truth. There was no turning back on this path, and justice for Daphne was his only motivation.

The Infiltration

As Sunday evening set in, the city sank into its usual quiet, unaware of the dark plans unfolding in its shadowed alleys. Aris and Myrto stood silently before Karras's building. It was imposing, its façade deceptively innocent, yet hiding secrets that could ruin lives.

Dressed in black and carrying the tools provided by their mysterious contact, they approached the back entrance. Myrto pulled a thin tool from her bag and started working on the lock. After a few minutes, a soft click sounded—the door was open. They exchanged a final glance, and Aris entered first, with Myrto close behind.

Inside, the building was completely silent. The lights were off, the only illumination coming from the faint glow of street lamps through the windows. They moved slowly, the only sounds were their breaths and the soft echo of their footsteps down the hallway.

Aris had prepared himself for this night, but the intensity of the moment was overwhelming. Each step brought him closer to answers—and to a danger he couldn't fully predict.

Reaching Karras's office, Myrto took out the map and examined it closely. "The financial records should be in a hidden safe behind the bookshelf," she whispered, pointing to the large bookcase covering the wall.

Aris began scanning the shelves, searching for a mechanism. Soon, he found a small lever hidden behind some books. He pulled it, and with a quiet creak, the bookshelf shifted, revealing a metal door.

"It's here," he said, his voice thick with tension.

Myrto crouched and started working on the safe's lock. Minutes dragged on, their anxiety mounting as they knew time was short. Finally, the safe opened, revealing a series of folders packed with financial documents, contracts, and accounts showing illegal transactions and payments to members of the organization.

"This is enough to bring them down," Myrto said with satisfaction as they began gathering the files.

Suddenly, footsteps echoed down the hallway. Someone was approaching, heavy and unrelenting. Aris and Myrto froze, realizing that if they were found here, they'd be in serious danger. Without another thought, they shut the safe and slipped behind the bookshelf, hoping they wouldn't be detected.

A man entered the office, his gaze cold and scrutinizing. He was one of Karras's henchmen, and his eyes scanned the room suspiciously. He lingered for a moment, taking a slow, methodical look around before turning and leaving, allowing them to finally exhale in relief.

"We have to get out now," Myrto whispered, and Aris nodded. Gathering up the documents, they carefully slipped out of the office and made their way to the exit. The tension kept them on edge, and when they finally stepped outside, the cool night air felt liberating.

Walking toward the car, Aris looked at Myrto with a mix of satisfaction and concern. "We have everything we need to destroy them, but we know they'll come after us as soon as they realize what's happened."

Myrto nodded. "That's the risk. But justice for Daphne is worth it. We'll need to be careful from here on."

Aris looked down at the folders in his hands, filled with determination. "We'll expose them to the public. Everything they did to Daphne, all the secrets they've kept hidden for so long, will come to light."

As they moved away from the building, Aris felt, for the first time, that his revenge had taken shape. The fight ahead would be challenging, but now he had the means to win it.

The Plan for Revelation

Aris and Myrto spent the rest of the night analyzing the documents they had gathered. They were filled with evidence of illegal transactions, under-the-table deals, and secret contracts linking Karras to other powerful figures in the city. It was the confirmation they needed: Daphne had uncovered something massive—something that, if exposed, would bring down the entire network.

Myrto, looking over the papers, turned to Aris. "These documents are enough to create an earthquake in the business and political world. But we need to plan how to reveal them without putting ourselves in immediate danger. These people won't hesitate to eliminate us."

Aris leaned over the documents, thinking deeply. "We need a way to make this information public, to people who will support us and ensure the case isn't buried. We might need to approach a high-profile journalist with experience in uncovering corruption."

Myrto nodded. "I know someone who could help. Anna Leventi is a journalist who's exposed numerous corruption scandals. If we hand these documents to her, she'll publish them, making it difficult for Karras's organization to cover it up."

The next day, they arranged a meeting with Anna at a quiet café away from the city center. Anna was a dynamic woman, with a sharp gaze and the confidence of someone who had seen it all.

Aris explained the story and showed her the documents. She studied them silently, her expression focused, and when she looked up, her determination was clear. "If this information goes public, it will shake up the city. But we need to be careful; Karras and his associates won't just stand by."

Aris nodded. "We know that, but we're willing to take the risk. Daphne deserves justice."

Anna smiled. "We'll need a solid plan to ensure your safety. I'll work with my team to prepare the publication, and we'll organize a way to keep you protected."

The following week was filled with preparations. Anna and her team worked tirelessly, verifying every piece of evidence and creating a detailed dossier to hand over to the authorities simultaneously with the publication. Aris and Myrto, hidden in a safe location, waited for the right moment.

On the day of the publication, the story hit the front pages of every newspaper and dominated television news. The revelations about Karras's network and the illegal activities he controlled shocked the public, and the city's society began demanding justice.

Karras and his associates tried to hide, but the evidence was irrefutable, and the pressure mounted. The authorities were forced to launch an investigation, and one by one, members of the organization were arrested.

Watching the events unfold on television, Aris felt a deep sense of satisfaction and vindication. He looked at Myrto, who was watching him with a faint smile. This was the moment he had been waiting for—the moment Daphne would finally find peace.

In the days that followed, the city was abuzz with talk of the scandal. Karras and his organization had been exposed, and the consequences were severe. Many of those involved in the illegal network scrambled to escape, while others tried to salvage whatever influence they could.

Aris and Myrto knew their work was done. Revenge had been served, and the truth had been brought to light. Though their journey had been filled with pain and turmoil, the outcome gave them the peace they had been seeking.

As they walked together through the city streets, no longer needing to hide, Myrto looked at him and said, "Daphne would be proud of you. You gave her justice."

Aris nodded, gazing at the sunset that bathed the city in golden light. The revenge was complete, but the sense of justice ran deep and steady. Holding Myrto's hand, he knew he could finally move forward.

A New Beginning

The days following the revelations were filled with change. The city was shaken by the scandal, and the fallout was sweeping. Karras and several members of the organization had been arrested, and investigations continued to expose the hidden power structures that had controlled the city's life for years.

Aris watched the developments, feeling a sense of justice but also an emptiness. He had devoted every part of himself to vindicating Daphne, and now that the journey was over, he knew it was time to find peace within himself.

Myrto was by his side every step of the way. With her, he had found an unexpected companionship, and through their shared mission, he had seen something more. Their relationship had started with doubt and suspicion, but trust and their shared quest had bonded them in a way he couldn't ignore.

One day, they decided to visit Daphne's grave. Standing before her memory, Aris felt a wave of sorrow but also gratitude. He had found the strength to uncover the truth, and her vindication was the gift he owed her.

Myrto stood beside him, placing a small white rose on the grave. "Daphne was brave," she whispered. "Her truth was the strength that brought us here."

Aris turned to her. "And you were brave. You stayed with me when everything seemed impossible. Because of you, I was able to complete this journey."

Myrto smiled softly. "Life is full of hard choices, Aris. But sometimes, through pain and loss, we find our path."

Aris took a deep breath, feeling the weight of revenge lift from his shoulders. He knew that, despite the sadness, it was time to move on. With Myrto, he could build a new life, free from anger and the thirst for vengeance.

As they walked away from the grave, Aris looked back one last time, bidding farewell to Daphne and the pain of the past. He was ready to start fresh, to discover a new reality beside a woman who had stood by him when everything seemed empty.

And so, with his head held high and his heart lighter, he took the first step toward his new life, knowing that he had finally found the peace he had been searching for.

Aris was adjusting to his new life. The void left by loss and revenge was beginning to fill with new experiences, relationships, and a peace he hadn't felt in a long time. The truth had been revealed, justice had been served, but most importantly, he had freed himself from the need for vengeance.

His relationship with Myrto continued to deepen, no longer just a bond born of shared trials but a profound companionship. Myrto was there, not only as an ally but now as a friend and partner—a devoted presence who helped him see the future with optimism.

One day, as they sat at a small café enjoying the city's sunlight, Myrto turned to him with a smile and said, "Now that it's all over, how about a fresh start? Something that brings us joy and creation."

Aris looked at her, surprised but thrilled by the suggestion. The idea of something new captivated him, and he knew this moment was his chance to leave behind all that had once held him captive.

"I'd love that," he replied, holding her hand. "Maybe it's time to start something of our own, something that fills our lives with the real and meaningful things we've discovered."

With their plans now revolving around a life free from intrigue and dark secrets, Aris and Myrto decided to create a small venture together, focusing on helping others find their own peace and truth. They envisioned a sanctuary for people who had faced similar trials and needed a place to heal.

The process was slow but deeply fulfilling. Together, they designed a retreat—a space for healing and renewal, where guests could escape life's struggles and rediscover themselves. This vision brought them even closer, and Aris felt that this endeavor was his own redemption, a way to honor Daphne's memory.

Months later, the sanctuary was ready to welcome its first visitors. The rooms radiated simplicity and warmth, with small nooks for reflection and rest. Aris and Myrto, along with a team of dedicated partners, had created a place that exuded peace and safety.

As Aris looked around at their accomplishment, he knew this was the life he wanted to live. Revenge had given way to creation, and sorrow had transformed into strength for something positive.

At the end of the day, as the sun set behind the mountains, Myrto stood beside him, looking at him with love and pride. "We did it, Aris. We created something beautiful from this journey."

Aris embraced her, whispering, "Yes, we did. And I'm grateful for everything. Because of you, I found a way to move forward and live again."

With Myrto by his side, Aris knew that their journey was just beginning—not to seek revenge or uncover hidden truths, but to build a life filled with hope and love.

A New Chapter

As the weeks passed, the sanctuary that Aris and Myrto had created began to gain recognition. People who had been hurt, who carried their own stories of sorrow and loss, started to find in this place a refuge—a space where they could heal and rediscover hope. Through this new mission, Aris felt more alive and fulfilled with each passing day.

One afternoon, as he stepped out of the main hall, a woman approached him. Her eyes were red from crying, but a faint smile of gratitude lit up her face.

"Thank you," she said in a trembling voice. "Thanks to this place, I've found the peace I've been searching for all these years. I don't know how to express it, but I feel free again."

Aris felt his heart swell with gratitude. Every soul finding its way in the sanctuary was a confirmation that his work had meaning. He looked at her warmly and replied, "This place exists to help people like you. You are safe here, and we're all here for you."

As she walked away, he felt Myrto's hand on his shoulder. Myrto, always by his side, shared these moments with him, her gaze filled with pride and love.

"You see? You've accomplished something truly special, Aris," she said with a smile. "Every life we help is a little miracle."

Aris returned her smile. "I couldn't have done it without you, Myrto. You helped me leave the past behind and build something new. And for the first time, I feel genuinely happy."

Days later, as they watched the sunset together, Aris shared a dream that had been simmering within him. "I'd love to expand this work to other cities. To create sanctuaries in places that need hope and healing."

Myrto listened intently, her eyes shining with excitement. "That would be wonderful, Aris. The change we've made here can reach everywhere, and together, we can help even more people."

Their idea took shape and quickly became a new vision for their future. They dedicated themselves to building a network of sanctuaries, aiming to provide support to anyone who needed it, in every corner of the country.

The challenges were many, but their strength and love for what they were doing propelled them forward. Over time, their work became known nationwide, and the community they had created was no longer just a shelter; it had grown into a movement of hope and healing, inspiring thousands.

Aris and Myrto had finally found peace and purpose, and their journey had turned into a life filled with giving, hope, and love. And as time passed, each day brought them closer to fulfilling their dream—to make the world a little better for all those in need of a second chance, just as they themselves had received.

...or so they believed, until then.

Traces of Betrayal

Aris was embracing his new life, filled with hope and plans for the future, but small things began to unsettle him. These were subtle hints—little details he might have easily dismissed as accidents or coincidences. Yet something inside him wouldn't rest.

The first sign came one afternoon when he overheard a conversation by chance. Sitting in a café while waiting for Myrto, he caught fragments of a hushed discussion about Karras and his underground network. The man was speaking in a low voice, as if afraid someone might overhear. Aris leaned in just enough to catch the words, and what he heard sent a chill through him:

"They set up an intricate plan to bring him down, used every tactic... even got close to people he should never have trusted."

Aris felt his pulse quicken, but he told himself it was probably nothing. Still, the seed of doubt had been planted.

In the days that followed, Aris noticed more odd behaviors. Myrto often disappeared in the evenings, her explanations vague. She had always been open with him, sharing even the smallest details, but now she avoided conversations about the past or her connections to certain people.

One night, unable to sleep as his mind circled with questions, he decided to glance through her things—not out of distrust, but out of a nagging worry. In her bag, he found a small notebook with notes on people tied to Karras. The names were familiar, but the comments beside them hinted at meetings and agreements he hadn't known about.

That night, Aris couldn't sleep. He started to wonder if Myrto had really been truthful about her past. Perhaps there were connections she hadn't mentioned, ties she had kept hidden from him.

As the days passed, the signs grew harder to ignore. Myrto seemed to have a mysterious line of communication she refused to explain. Once, Aris caught her on the phone with someone, abruptly ending the call as soon as he entered the room. Her face held a tension he hadn't seen before.

"Who was that?" he asked.

"Oh, no one, just an old friend. They were just asking about something trivial," she replied with a smile that seemed slightly forced.

As much as he wanted to believe her, something deep inside told him Myrto was hiding things she didn't want him to uncover. The thought left him feeling that the dream they had built together was beginning to unravel.

Finally, one night, he decided to follow her. He watched as she met with an unknown man in a secluded café. Keeping his distance, he listened carefully, catching fragments of their conversation.

"It's time to finish the plan," the man said with a tone of finality. "Aris is close to discovering the last piece we need."

Myrto looked shaken but agreed. "I didn't expect it to turn out this way... it's gotten harder than I imagined. I promised I wouldn't hurt him, but... I don't have a choice."

Aris felt the ground fall away beneath him. Myrto, the woman he had believed loved him, had been part of a plot against him from the beginning. He knew he had to keep up the act, pretending he knew nothing, to buy time and find all the answers.

Returning home, anger and grief consumed him, yet he resolved to stay silent. He wanted to see her reveal herself, to make her confess the truth. From that night on, he was ready for the final reckoning, determined to give her the chance to explain—or to pay the price for her betrayal.

The Revelation of the Plan

The days passed in tense silence for Aris. Myrto tried to maintain her usual warmth and smile, but Aris could see the subtle signs betraying her nerves. Pretending he hadn't noticed anything, he began observing her every move, gathering evidence of her betrayal.

One night, after she had fallen asleep, he decided to check her phone. He knew it was a breach of trust, but there was no trust left between them. When he opened her recent messages, his breath caught.

The messages were coded, but he understood enough to see they were about him. Words like "target" and "plan" appeared repeatedly, along with instructions Myrto was supposed to follow. Karras's name surfaced again and again, and the instructions were clear: Myrto was to win Aris's trust, coaxing him to reveal everything he knew about the organization so they could trap him.

Aris felt his anger rise, but he forced himself to stay calm. He needed time to decide how to respond. He knew he should give her a chance to explain, but he wanted her to expose herself, to confront him with the truth.

The next day, Aris suggested they take a walk to the place where their shared dream had begun—the sanctuary. Myrto, unaware of what he had discovered, agreed happily. During the drive, Aris gently prodded her about her past, pretending he was simply curious.

"You could say it all started with a series of coincidences," Myrto replied, her voice calm and confident. "Life often leads us in directions we never expect."

Her answer was composed, but Aris could see a faint hint of nervousness in her eyes. After a while, he pressed her a little more.

"Myrto, let's say someone was using me, trying to trap me. Would you tell me?" he asked, watching her closely.

She froze momentarily but quickly regained her composure. "Aris, why would you ask something like that? You and I… we've left the past behind."

Her response confirmed for him that the web was deeper than he had imagined. He stayed silent, waiting to see if she would reveal anything more. He knew the moment of reckoning was drawing near, and though anger simmered within him, he wanted to be sure he had all the answers before confronting her fully.

The Hidden Key

In the days that followed, Aris found himself diving back into memories of his life with Daphne, as if something hidden lay beneath their shared moments and conversations. Myrto's unexpected betrayal had shaken him, pushing him to reconsider everything he thought he knew.

One evening, alone in his study, he picked up Daphne's diary—something he'd held onto like a cherished keepsake. As he leafed through the pages, familiar phrases leapt out at him—little, cryptic things she used to say that had once seemed romantic or playful. Now, though, they felt charged with new meaning.

"Our secret lies in the heart, and the heart has its own paths," one line read. It was a phrase they'd shared often, like a private joke. But now, it seemed more like a hidden message—a clue she'd left behind without him realizing.

He began to wonder if Daphne had created a hidden code, phrases only he would recognize—words that, pieced together in the right way, could unlock something much bigger.

As the idea took shape, Aris felt both a thrill and a strange sense of urgency. If his instincts were correct, Daphne had entrusted him, unknowingly, with access to something powerful—and dangerous. Maybe she'd left him the key to documents or secrets that could unravel Karras's web.

Rereading the diary, he began to reconstruct this "code." Each phrase, each word, seemed to click into place, like pieces of a puzzle he hadn't known he was solving. These weren't just words—they were part of something he'd memorized through love, not realizing the weight they carried.

That evening, Myrto was already home, her gaze betraying a hidden unease. Aris, pretending he knew nothing, suggested they talk about everything they'd been through. "You know, Myrto," he said, "after all this, I feel like Daphne left me something valuable, something I need to uncover."

Myrto tried to mask the tension in her eyes and asked with forced indifference, "What do you mean?"

"Maybe it's a series of memories we shared. A code that only she and I could understand," he replied, watching her closely.

Unable to keep up the facade, Myrto suggested they go somewhere quiet to talk. She looked anxious, and Aris knew this was the moment when the truth would finally come out.

The next day, they met in a secluded spot, far from prying eyes. In a moment of honesty, Myrto began to explain the plan that had been set in motion against him from the start.

"Aris, Daphne gained access to highly valuable information—confidential files containing details about Karras's entire organization. Your relationship was her cover, her protection. She left you these hidden keys, these words and codes, in ways you wouldn't suspect. And I... I was part of the plan. They sent me to get close to you, to make you reveal what you unknowingly held all along."

Aris looked at her, his gaze filled with anger and disappointment. "So this whole relationship, every moment we shared... it was all just to extract information from me?"

Myrto lowered her head, guilt washing over her. "At first, yes. It was my duty. But then... I fell in love with you. What we have is real for me, Aris, but I can't change the past. You're free to condemn me."

Aris remained silent, feeling the weight of betrayal settle in. All he knew now was that this code, this hidden truth Daphne had left him, was the key to bringing down Karras's entire organization. And even though he'd lost all trust in Myrto, he was determined to uncover the secrets Daphne had left for him.

In Search of the Hidden Code

Filled with a newfound resolve, Aris returned to his office with a clear purpose. Revenge had taken on a different form, and now, the only thing standing between him and justice was the hidden code Daphne had left him—a secret he unknowingly possessed, woven into phrases and moments from their relationship. It was a puzzle only the two of them could piece together.

He began to recall every word Daphne had said, every subtle smile, every seemingly innocent comment, each one now carrying the possibility of deeper meaning. He jotted down key phrases and words that came to mind:

- "The heart has its own secrets."
- "Truth hides in the smallest things."
- "What we don't say holds the most power."

Each phrase seemed to form pieces of an unseen map, a path he needed to follow to unlock the secret Daphne had entrusted to him without his even knowing.

Days passed, and Aris moved forward slowly, carefully linking each phrase and connection that might offer a hint to the code. He kept his mission concealed, avoiding even Myrto, as he knew he couldn't yet see her as an ally. Her betrayal had cut deep, yet he realized that, ironically, she might be the only person who could truly help him solve this puzzle.

One evening, after reading through Daphne's journal countless times, he noticed a phrase that stood out from the rest. Daphne had once written to him:

"If anything goes wrong, remember our first date and the promise you made me."

Aris paused, feeling the weight of those words settle around him. This memory, once cherished, now seemed like a clue that could lead him directly to the truth.

Aris remembered their first date: a night filled with innocence and hope, where he had promised Daphne he would protect her from any danger. It was one of those moments when his words had flowed out naturally, warm and devoted. Now, though, that promise seemed to hold a hidden meaning. Could it be a hint to the code he sought?

As he reread the phrase, he felt that perhaps there were other hidden layers to her words, subtle clues that might reveal the answer he needed.

That evening, Myrto, noticing Aris's intense focus in recent days, sensed that he had discovered something significant. She had tried to speak to him, but he continued to keep his distance. Determined, she decided to take the first step to show that she truly wanted to be by his side—to help reveal the truth and bring down Karras.

"Aris," she said one afternoon, approaching him carefully. "I know it's hard for you to trust me again, but... if we try to solve this puzzle together, maybe we can get closer to the truth you're looking for. If we think of it as a game between Karras and me, then maybe I stand a better chance of deceiving him."

Aris looked at her thoughtfully. He knew she was right. Karras's power was far greater than he had imagined, and perhaps Myrto, with her insider knowledge of his tactics and tricks, was the only person who could help him succeed.

They decided to work together. Aris began explaining the subtle cues he had noticed in Daphne's phrases, and together they started analyzing every word, every hint, searching for patterns and coded messages. Myrto, drawing from her knowledge of Karras's system, explained how criminal organizations often embedded codes in everyday language—phrases that would seem completely ordinary to anyone else.

One evening, as they combed through a letter Daphne had sent him, Myrto noticed something unusual.

"Aris, look at this," she said, pointing to a specific paragraph. "It reads like a typical message, but these words... it's almost like they're hinting at something else."

The choice of words in that paragraph revealed an unusual pattern—a sequence that could easily be a password or some form of encryption. Analyzing the order of the words, Aris and Myrto noticed that every second word followed a specific sequence. They realized that this could be the beginning of the code they'd been searching for.

As they drew closer to deciphering the code, news reached them that Karras had been released from prison. Myrto knew immediately what that meant: he would track them down soon and force them to give up the information he sought. Karras was determined to ensure that Myrto had obtained the code from Aris.

"This is our only way to stay ahead of him," Myrto said with a calm resolve. "We need to make Karras believe we have the code and that we'll hand it over—if he agrees to leave us alone."

Aris looked at her with newfound respect, realizing just how deeply she had committed herself to this fight. He understood now that Myrto was no longer an enemy; she was his only ally on this dangerous path.

Pieces of the Puzzle

As Aris and Myrto delved further into decoding the cryptic messages, their relationship grew stronger through the tension and uncertainties each new discovery brought. Every phrase they unraveled drew them closer to the truth—and to the danger lurking around it.

Aris began recalling even more details of his past with Daphne. She had her own way of communicating hidden messages to him—sometimes through her notes, other times through casual conversation. He remembered how she would often say, "The most important secrets are always hidden where you least expect them."

One day, while going through Daphne's old notes, he noticed something in an anniversary card she'd once given him. It was filled with symbolic language and phrases that had seemed innocent at the time, but now took on a new significance. One line, in particular, stood out: "Where night meets day." Was she referring to a specific location? A meeting spot that only the two of them would know?

Just as the pieces seemed to start falling into place, a new player entered the scene. Stefanos, a former associate of Daphne's, had reached out to Aris, claiming he could no longer keep the secrets she had confided in him. Aris and Myrto found themselves waiting in an old café, as Stefanos had suggested. Though curious, Aris couldn't shake a sense of apprehension; Daphne had never mentioned this associate. How had Stefanos earned her trust deeply enough to be part of her hidden plan?

Stefanos arrived shortly after. He was a man in his early forties, of average build, with a calm yet commanding presence. His gaze held a distant, somber quality, as though he'd witnessed things he would rather forget. Dressed in a black coat, he approached their table with a faint smile—a smile that suggested he knew far more than he was letting on.

"Aris," Stefanos began, extending his hand, "Daphne spoke of you often. She told me about the bond you shared." He then turned to Myrto, offering her a polite but scrutinizing nod, as though assessing her.

Aris eyed him skeptically but decided to listen. "Tell us, Stefanos. How exactly did you know Daphne? And why should I believe you were more than just a colleague?"

Stefanos took a deep breath, leaning closer and glancing around to ensure no one was watching. "Daphne and I met about four years ago at a series of cybersecurity seminars. She was passionate about her work and her ideals, and I soon realized she was far more than just a skilled professional."

He paused, looking down at the table as if piecing together old memories. "After a few encounters, she confided something serious in me. She'd uncovered critical information about Karras's organization and its criminal dealings. She knew that by exposing them, she would become a target, so she started putting together a meticulous plan to safeguard that information—just in case anything happened to her."

Aris listened closely, the details grounding Stefanos's story in a way that felt all too real. "And why did she trust you to help her?" he asked, his voice low but firm.

Stefanos offered a faint smile, one touched by bitterness. "I had my own reasons for wanting to see Karras's empire fall. He destroyed something precious to me once, and I wanted him to pay for it. Daphne knew this and believed I could help her. I worked for a cybersecurity company with access to technology that allowed us to hide data in various locations, keeping it out of Karras's reach."

Myrto, watching Stefanos intently, asked, "And what do you know about the code? How does it connect to the evidence she hid?"

Leaning in closer, Stefanos looked at them with a cryptic expression. "Daphne knew the code had to be more than just a set of characters. She wanted it to be something only the two of you would understand—a pattern hidden in phrases and memories. She created a combination of four keywords, each linked to a place that held meaning for you both. You, Aris, are the key because only you know these locations and what they represent."

As the weight of Stefanos's words sank in, Aris realized that Daphne had devised a deeply personal way to protect her secrets—a treasure hunt that only he could solve.

Stefanos continued, "Daphne left specific instructions to safeguard this information. She was clear: if anyone ever tried to extract the code from you, only you could know how to piece it together. It's a puzzle rooted in your memories. And most importantly," he added, glancing at Myrto, "Daphne believed that if things went awry, you'd need a partner. Someone to rely on."

Aris met Myrto's gaze, recognizing her significance despite the initial betrayal. Daphne, in her unique and unpredictable way, had created a safety net that now bound them all.

As Stefanos left, he gave them one last directive. "Seek out those four places. In each one, Daphne left a piece of the code. You'll need to recall your moments together there, Aris, and remember the phrases she shared with you. Only then can you uncover the truth."

With a newfound sense of responsibility and resolve, Aris felt the weight of the journey ahead. Myrto, standing by his side, was ready to face whatever lay in their path.

Yet the threat of Karras loomed close. They knew their time was limited, and as Aris's confidence grew, Myrto understood that they had entered the final stage of their pursuit for justice. The challenges were becoming more dangerous by the day, strengthening their alliance, as their search for truth became a fight for survival.

The First Clue

Guided by Stefanos's directions, Aris and Myrto set off to uncover the four key locations. They now understood that each place would hold a part of the code that Daphne had hidden, connected in a way only they could decipher through shared memories.

Back in the office, Aris and Myrto reflected on Stefanos's words, which resonated in their minds. They knew they had to find four places—four locations encoded in the moments and phrases Daphne had carefully left behind. Aris began to recall places that had held special meaning in their relationship, moments that had left an imprint.

"We need to think of places that truly mattered to us—places where she might have hidden something of true significance," Aris said, his voice filled with thoughtfulness.

Myrto nodded, her eyes never leaving his face, sensing the weight of this task and the memories it brought back. "If we start from the beginning, what's the first place that comes to mind? Somewhere she would choose to hide something important?"

Closing his eyes, Aris sifted through memories. "The first night we spent together, at that beach outside the city... Daphne said something to me then, as if she was trying to share a deeper meaning beyond the romance of the moment."

"The beach, then," Myrto responded with resolve. "We'll start there."

The drive to the secluded beach was quiet, the silence between them dense with unspoken thoughts. The setting sun cast its last golden rays over the landscape, evoking a flood of memories for Aris—moments of hope and connection now tinged with urgency. A mix of nostalgia and trepidation stirred within him, while Myrto, watching him, wondered how she could help him unlock the memories of that night.

"Aris," she asked gently, her voice barely above a whisper, "do you remember anything specific from that night? Something she said to you?"

Aris paused, looking at the waves crashing against the rocks. "She told me, 'What's most precious isn't what we see, but what we carry in our hearts.' Back then, I thought it was just romantic, a bit of a joke. But now... it feels like a riddle."

Myrto stayed silent, pondering the weight of that phrase. "Maybe," she suggested, "Daphne meant something hidden, something we don't see with our eyes."

Encouraged by her words, Aris began to comb through the area, examining every detail with care. Among the rocks, his fingers traced a narrow crevice, discovering something lodged within—as if someone had intentionally placed it there long ago. Without hesitation, he reached down and pulled out an old, weathered box.

Opening it, he discovered a card with a few simple words written on it: *Light, Silence, Sacrifice, Memory*. The words seemed simple but carried a weight he could sense deeply. Each one felt like it represented a profound and personal element of his relationship with Daphne, crafted to protect the truth.

Myrto, noticing how absorbed Aris was, placed a supportive hand on his shoulder, grounding him in the gravity of the moment. Aris noted down the words, feeling a surge of energy within him. This was the first piece of the puzzle...

On their way back from the beach, Aris and Myrto reflected on the next location. Myrto gently guided his thoughts, her voice calm and reassuring.

"Think, Aris. If the first word, *Light*, led us to the beach, what could be connected to the word *Silence*?"

Aris pondered for a moment, his brow furrowing as memories came rushing back. "Maybe an art gallery. There's a place Daphne used to take me—a quiet, almost sacred place for her. There's a painting there, a piece that captures shadows, and she once told me that shadows always hide something valuable."

Myrto smiled, a spark of excitement lighting her eyes. "Then that must be it. Let's go there—it might hold the next piece of the puzzle."

With renewed determination, they set their course for the gallery, both feeling the pull of Daphne's mystery. Each step they took brought them closer to unveiling the hidden truth she had left behind, and they knew there could be no turning back.

The Second Clue

The next day found Aris and Myrto at the art gallery—a place where he and Daphne would come to discuss life, dreams, and everything in between. As they wandered among the paintings, Aris's eyes fell on one particular piece: a painting of shadows intertwining, shapeless yet somehow meaningful. Daphne had once remarked, "Shadows always hide something precious." At the time, it seemed like a passing thought, but now, those words felt loaded with purpose.

The painting still hung in its usual spot. Observing it more closely, Aris noticed a slight imperfection in the frame, something he hadn't seen before. He took a step back, analyzing every detail. Then, with a steady breath, he reached into the gap in the frame and pulled out a small folded note. Opening it, he read: "What's hidden is also protected." Another clue to the nature of the code.

Standing beside him, Myrto looked at him with admiration. "Perhaps she wanted to show you that the code is something to be safeguarded. Each step brings us closer," she said gently.

Aris gave her a grateful look, realizing that he couldn't have gotten this far alone.

After their time at the gallery, they decided to pause and consider their next move. The word "Sacrifice" weighed on them, as it was difficult to tie it to any particular place.

Noticing Aris's pensive expression, Myrto offered, "Could it be somewhere that holds memories of difficult choices?"

Suddenly, Aris remembered a church on the outskirts of the city, where he and Daphne had once shared a deep conversation about the sacrifices they'd make for each other.

Myrto looked at him with intrigue. "Tell me about that moment. What happened at the church?"

Aris was silent for a moment, lost in thought, before he began to explain. "We were going through a rough patch, full of doubts about staying together. One day, without planning it, we ended up at that church. Daphne was visibly troubled, and she told me, 'Relationships demand sacrifices, and every sacrifice has its price. But if it's for something greater, then it's worth the risk.' At that moment, it felt like a promise—a bond that would connect us, even if circumstances turned against us."

Myrto listened intently, sensing the depth of that memory and how powerfully Daphne's presence lingered in Aris's life.

"Let's go to the church, then," Myrto said, resolved to accompany him on this emotional journey. She understood that each place they uncovered wasn't just a piece of the code but a way for Aris to rediscover the most profound layers of his bond with Daphne. Each stop was as much about the memories as it was about the secrets they now held.

Aris nodded, feeling a surge of mixed emotions—anticipation, nostalgia, and perhaps a touch of apprehension. The church was a place woven with memories, and revisiting it felt like stepping back into an intimate past he hadn't expected to relive. But as he took a steadying breath, he realized that these fragments of the past, painful as they might be, were the keys to the truth he now sought.

Together, they set off, ready to uncover what awaited them at the next stop on this journey of revelations and reconciliations.

The Third Location

When they arrived at the church, it was late afternoon. Sunlight streamed through the stained-glass windows, casting colorful reflections on the stone walls and filling the space with a sense of reverence and awe. The church was empty, its silence inviting them to uncover the hidden truths within.

Aris walked slowly toward the altar, recalling how he and Daphne had sat there that night, talking about the sacrifices their relationship required. He stopped in front of the pew where Daphne had rested her hand that night when she had made that promise, and a bittersweet smile appeared on his face.

"It was right here," he murmured softly, "where I told her that no matter what happened, I'd make any sacrifice for her. She knew how hard that was for me, but she accepted it."

Myrto stepped closer, her eyes scanning the area around the pew, searching for anything that might have been left behind. Beneath the seat, almost hidden, she found a small wooden plaque. Carefully, she pulled it out and read the words etched upon it:

"Faith, Purpose, Trust."

These words seemed simple, yet Aris knew they held a deeper meaning. "Our faith, our purpose, our trust—they were always the foundation of my bond with Daphne," he whispered, holding the plaque as if it were sacred.

Myrto looked at him with empathy. "Maybe each of these words represents something that held special significance in your relationship. Finding the code isn't just about numbers or words, Aris. It's also about rediscovering what that relationship meant to you."

Aris realized that each place they visited was bringing them closer to the truth—not only the truth of the code but also of everything Daphne had tried to leave behind for them.

With three locations now clearly identified—the beach for "Light," the gallery for "Silence," and the church for "Sacrifice"—the last word, "Memory," called them to think more intimately. Myrto looked at Aris, grasping the depth of what this final word represented.

"Memory... it's tied to everything you remember of her. Is there a place that holds the most profound memories of her?" she asked softly.

Aris thought for a moment, then remained silent, the realization sinking in. "Her home. That's where she lived, where she left traces of herself. Every memory we shared, the moments of her life, and the day we said goodbye are all bound to that place."

Myrto nodded in agreement. "Then that's where 'Memory' lies—at her home, among all the memories she left behind."

The Fourth Point

Arriving at her house, Aris felt an overwhelming wave of emotions wash over him. The house was filled with Daphne's presence—in the little details they had shared, the objects she had touched, the moments they had lived. It was a place of memory; every corner and nook held traces of her essence.

Myrto followed him quietly into the house, observing the objects around her with respectful silence. Aris led her to Daphne's study, a warm, inviting space where she would write, study, and reflect.

"This was her favorite place," he said. "She would spend hours here, pouring her thoughts and dreams into words. Everything that mattered to her was here."

On the desk, beside a photo of the two of them, lay an old, worn notebook. Aris opened it carefully, reading Daphne's words, which seemed written with the knowledge that he would someday find them.

On the final page was a simple line: "Memory connects us to the past and guides us toward the future." Next to the phrase, in small, fancy handwriting and written in red ink, were the letters: R, V, O, E and F. Aris stared at them, confused. These letters, almost like they were meant just for him, formed a puzzle—a series of clues that needed to be solved.

Thinking back to what he had found at the four places he had visited, the letters started to feel familiar. He remembered their first conversation at the art gallery, the nights they spent together at the beach, their talks at the house, and the quiet moments in the church where they spoke without words, only glances. Each place, each special memory, had given him a small but important phrase.

As his mind wandered through these memories, he noticed that the letters weren't placed randomly. It was like they were arranged in a specific order that could unlock the answer to the puzzle. He began to rearrange them, saying them over and over, trying to find the right combination. It felt like all the messages Daphne had left were coming back to him, leading him bit by bit to the hidden word.

Aris stared at the letters with intense concentration, trying to find the right arrangement, the correct combination that would give them meaning. R, V, O, E, F. Each time he shuffled them, they formed words that made no logical sense, as if something vital was eluding him. He began to whisper them softly, testing each possible combination:

"Vore... Fero... Refov..." But each time, the result seemed wrong, desperately far from the answer he was searching for.

With growing frustration, he tried again, rearranging the letters, skipping some, adding others in his mind, until finally, he stumbled upon something that felt closer to the truth: "For..."

This word, although almost correct, still felt incomplete. Something was missing to make it whole. It became clear that one or two more letters, a final addition, were needed to give the word its complete form. And then he realized he had to add another "E" and one final "R" to make it definitive.

When he added the second "E" and the final "R," everything fell into place, as if he had unlocked the last door to the truth:

"Forever."

The word was there, ready to give him the answer he had been searching for so long. On his own, he had found the missing pieces, connected the dots, and reached Daphne's final promise – the promise that would remain true forever.

This word, revealed through the letters, seemed to be Daphne's final, timeless promise. With precision and method, she had left behind these signs to guide him, to show him the truth she had always wanted to share with him. This word was not only the solution to the puzzle; it was a symbol of their relationship, of her faith in him, and of their enduring connection, regardless of the tragic end that separated them.

The feeling of completion overwhelmed him. Through those small, scattered letters, Daphne had left him the most important message. The message that called him to continue, to believe in the truth and the power of their love.

This word, filled with meanings and memories, was probably also the code they had been looking for. He looked at Myrto with tears in his eyes, feeling that this word was the strongest, deepest sign of love that Daphne had left him.

Aris felt his heart tighten. He had found the answer he was seeking, the final hidden phrase that Daphne had left him. He looked at Myrto with eyes full of emotion and determination.

"This is the code," he whispered, feeling that Daphne was there, with them.

The light, the truth, and the code were in their hands. And they knew that with it, they would close the circle that Daphne had opened, bringing final justice.

The Key to Truth

Aris and Myrto sat in front of Daphne's old computer, the dim light casting a tense atmosphere over the room. They had reached the final moment—the moment when the past would reveal all its secrets, and the truth would finally emerge. On the screen, a single message awaited: "Enter password."

With fingers trembling slightly, Aris took a deep breath and whispered, **"Forever,"** glancing at Myrto for reassurance. She gave him an encouraging nod, and he typed in the word—the last piece Daphne had left him, filled with meaning and love.

He pressed Enter. For a moment, the screen stayed dark, and then folders and files began to appear, each with coded names that hinted at the wealth of information Daphne had amassed.

"It's all here," Aris said, his voice thick with emotion. "Every proof, every detail of Karras's organization and their dirty dealings."

Myrto leaned closer, her gaze fixed on the files unfolding before them. They saw names they recognized: associates, financiers, even politicians entangled in Karras's web. Each file contained detailed records of his network's operations—evidence of money laundering, corruption, and threats against anyone who knew too much.

Opening one particular file, they stumbled upon something unexpected: a message from Daphne to Aris. The file, titled "For Aris," opened to reveal a video. Daphne appeared on the screen, her face calm, a knowing smile on her lips as if she'd always known this moment would come.

"Aris," she began, "if you're watching this, you've found the truth. I always knew you had the strength to reach this point, even if you didn't realize it yourself. I did everything I could to protect this information and ensure justice would be served. I knew you'd get here—with the right help."

Myrto, her eyes brimming with tears, squeezed Aris's hand, feeling the weight of Daphne's words. She knew Daphne had been guiding them even after her passing, laying the groundwork for the truth that was now coming to light.

Daphne continued, her voice steady. "What I want you to remember, Aris, is that nothing can ever extinguish the light of truth. Protect it, just as you protected our relationship."

Aris felt a tightness in his chest as the video ended, Daphne's image fading from the screen, leaving them holding everything they needed to bring down Karras.

"We don't have a choice anymore," Aris said finally, looking at Myrto. "We need to make this public. It's the only way to bring justice."

Doubt

The silence following Daphne's words weighed heavily, and Aris felt an unsettling tension filling him. Staring at the files on the screen, he tried to process all they had just uncovered. Yet something held him back from feeling any relief or sense of vindication.

He recalled the moment at Daphne's home—the final location where they'd found the code. Something in her study had caught his eye: a small silver box, adorned with an intricate chain, sitting in an unusual spot on her desk. He knew Daphne had always kept it in a specific place near her books, cherishing it as a family heirloom her mother had left her, imbuing it with symbolic meaning around faith and integrity.

But now, that box had been moved and lay open, its contents empty, exposed in a way that felt jarring. This detail nagged at him—not just the change in its placement but the symbolic emptiness it now presented. In Daphne's life, that box had always been kept closed, as though guarding a secret or a promise. It seemed deliberate, as if someone had left it there to communicate a final message.

This thought rooted itself deep in his mind, haunting him, though he chose not to mention it to Myrto. The absence of explanation and the intensity of his emotions made him hesitant to share his suspicions with her, even now, with the files in their possession. His trust was wavering, and he felt that something had yet to be fully revealed—the presence of that box seemed like a final warning, a silent nudge that the story wasn't over.

As Myrto watched him with a sense of relief for what they had uncovered, Aris found himself unable to focus. His mind kept circling back to whether he should tell her about the box or investigate on his own to understand its significance. He chose silence, attempting to concentrate on the evidence in front of them.

But deep down, he knew there was still a lingering darkness he couldn't ignore. Determined to return to Daphne's house alone, he made the excuse that he wanted to ensure they hadn't missed any files. He needed to see the box again, to confirm his suspicions and discover whether someone had betrayed not only Daphne but also the truth he was so desperately trying to unveil.

The night was well advanced when Aris found himself once again at Daphne's doorstep. The neighborhood was silent, with lights dimmed in the surrounding houses, leaving only shadows dancing on the walls. The air was cold, and his heart pounded with a mix of anxiety and anticipation.

He unlocked the door slowly, as if fearing that someone might hear him. The house was exactly as he and Myrto had left it, with Daphne's presence still lingering in every corner. But his focus was only on one thing—the silver box that had troubled him since he first noticed it.

He headed towards the study, his mind racing with questions. Why had the box been left open? Was it meant to convey a message he had yet to understand?

Reaching the desk, his gaze fell upon the box. He touched it gently, as though it were something fragile and sacred. Examining the interior, he found it empty, dark, as though something significant had been removed. The chain around the box bore a slight notch, as if it had been hastily broken.

A shiver ran through Aris. This box had been a symbol of trust for Daphne—a keepsake her mother had given her, with the promise to always keep it sealed, like a relic safeguarding an oath. The fact that someone had broken into it filled him with rage.

The Trace of Truth

As Aris studied the open box, a whirlwind of thoughts overwhelmed him. He knew this item was sacred to Daphne—a family heirloom symbolizing trust and her lasting memory. Whoever had opened it clearly believed they'd uncovered something precious—perhaps the code. Yet, as Aris examined the area around the box, his eyes landed on something peculiar.

Next to the box, lying as if it had fallen and shifted, was a small silver tag. He picked it up, examining it closely. It was something he'd seen many times before, yet he couldn't quite place to whom it belonged. The only thing he was certain of was that it felt familiar—the tag was wrapped in a piece of cord, with initials that had faded over time engraved upon it.

Setting it aside for now, Aris decided to focus on the suspicion that gnawed at him regarding Myrto. His doubts intensified, and each small detail seemed to reinforce the idea that perhaps Myrto had been collaborating with Karras all along.

Shadows of Suspicion

Aris couldn't shake the feeling that something was off about Myrto's behavior. From the start of their partnership, he had trusted her passion and commitment to the case, but as they neared the final revelation, his unease grew. Myrto seemed unusually eager, almost rushing toward an immediate conclusion. This haste made him suspect she might be hiding something.

He began recalling moments when she had shown knowledge of details he had never shared with her, as if she had somehow acquired the information on her own. During discussions about Karras, Myrto had hinted that she understood the organization's structure and operations, as though she had been following the case long before he involved her. At the time, he had attributed it to her intelligence, but now it felt like more than just sharp intuition.

Another red flag appeared when they began planning to hand over their evidence to the authorities. Myrto was insistent that they act swiftly, disregarding any risks of retaliation. Each time Aris raised concerns about caution and secure handling, Myrto seemed to react nervously, dodging the conversation. Her urgency felt like more than a drive for the truth—she seemed determined to ensure everything proceeded on her terms, and fast.

Shadows of Doubt

As Aris observed more and more signs, he found himself emotionally distancing from Myrto, noting the details and small hints he had previously overlooked. The closeness they had developed recently now seemed oddly artificial, even calculated. Reflecting on their early meetings, Aris recalled how Myrto always seemed to be a step ahead, as if she understood the significance of every move they made together. While he had tried to attribute this behavior to her passion for justice, something deep within him now sowed doubt.

Reviewing events, Aris began questioning her motives. There was a sequence of incidents that led him to suspect that Myrto might have her own hidden agenda—one she hadn't fully revealed to him. He felt trapped, sensing that if Myrto was indeed connected to Karras, she may have drawn him into her game, using him to access information she otherwise couldn't obtain.

Determined to probe further, Aris decided to ask subtle questions, hoping to gauge her reactions or detect any evasiveness. During one of their meetings, he asked, "Myrto, what exactly drove you to help in this case? I know you've seen things that aren't easy to bring to light."

For a brief moment, Myrto seemed caught off guard, but she quickly regained her composure. "Daphne was my friend, Aris. And... we all have our reasons to despise Karras."

Her response, though seemingly innocent, had a detached tone that only intensified his unease. As he began to discern a pattern in her reactions, Aris suspected that Myrto might be hiding more than she let on.

Aris started observing her closely, noticing small details in her expressions—subtle signs that suggested avoidance, a hint of a shadow that didn't fit the image he had of her. Over time, he came to view her as a possible adversary, and his trust eroded further.

Yet, the silver ID tag he had found by the box gnawed at him. It seemed unrelated to Myrto... Could it be, he wondered, that Myrto was merely a red herring, someone leading him to suspect a betrayal that didn't exist?

The Threat Rekindled

Karras's release hit like a bombshell. In the first hours of his newfound freedom, rage and a thirst for revenge consumed him. He had no intention of letting things be or forgetting the conviction that had cost him months behind bars. Word of Aris and Myrto's moves had reached him through his networks. Every piece of information he received about them—their collaboration, the files they held—kept him on high alert.

Karras summoned his most trusted men. Known for his influence and his ability to gather intelligence and eliminate threats with ease, his gaze was steely, filled with ruthless anger. His mind was focused on one thing: eliminating Aris and Myrto before they could reveal anything that would jeopardize everything he had built.

"I want you to find them," he said, his voice dripping with menace. "I know they have files that could hurt us. I won't allow anything to be made public, nor will I let them get near Stelios. I want them silenced... permanently."

His men nodded in obedience, fully aware of the gravity behind his words. Karras's vengeance knew no bounds, and he wouldn't hesitate to destroy anyone or anything standing in his way.

Rumors Spread

Meanwhile, Aris and Myrto heard about Karras's release. Aris's heart sank; he knew their time was now limited, and they couldn't afford even a moment of complacency. Karras wasn't someone who would let this situation go unpunished, and his looming presence made them realize they were sitting on a ticking bomb.

"Things are about to get more difficult," Myrto said, her voice calm despite the concern in her eyes, as she tried to keep her worry in check.

Aris looked at her, seeking reassurance in her eyes, though he wasn't entirely sure how they would move forward. "We know Karras won't leave anything to chance. This means we have to stay ten steps ahead."

Myrto moved closer to Aris, her grip on his hand firm and steady—a gesture that brought an unspoken sense of solidarity and closeness. "No matter what happens, we'll face it together. You're not alone in this."

This sense of support from Myrto strengthened him, and for a moment, the air between them thickened with emotions they had both kept suppressed all this time.

Karras, meanwhile, wasted no time. Seated in his office, he scrutinized the information he had gathered, fully aware that Aris and Myrto were not entirely unsuspecting. This knowledge drove him to craft a plan that was not only complex but ruthless. He needed a strategy with no loose ends, one that would lull Aris and Myrto into a false sense of security before stripping away any chance of escape.

Gathering his most ruthless men, Karras made it clear that failure was not an option. His goal wasn't just to monitor them but to deliver a final, crushing blow, ensuring that their files would never see the light of day.

"First, we'll make them think they're winning. Then, we'll destroy them," he said, his gaze filled with hatred. His men responded without a word—loyal to Karras and his interests, each one well aware of the consequences of betrayal or failure.

The Calm Before the Storm

The night was quiet, a gentle breeze stirring the trees and bringing a sense of peace. Aris and Myrto had returned to their hideaway, far from prying eyes and the dangers trailing them. Here, just for a moment, they could leave the tension behind and sink into something that felt nearly impossible under the circumstances: tranquility.

As they entered the room, they exchanged a look that held everything they couldn't put into words. It was a look of need, understanding, and longing for a moment without fear. Myrto smiled softly, placing her hand on Aris's face, her fingers tracing gently along his jawline. He felt his heart beat faster.

"For tonight, let's forget everything," she whispered, her voice calm and grounding.

Aris nodded, feeling the weight of her words. He gently pulled her close, and as he looked into her eyes, it was as if he could see past the darkness surrounding them—a glimmer of hope worth holding on to. Their touch was slow and intimate, as if they were discovering each other in a new way, leaving behind every doubt and fear.

Determined to create a memory strong enough to carry them through the days ahead, they let themselves draw closer, the room filling with the warmth and intensity of the moment. The lights were dim, casting soft shadows on the walls, and the moonlight poured in through the window, highlighting their silhouettes.

As Myrto wrapped her arms around Aris's shoulders, they both felt the profound sense of trust between them. The uncertainty that had haunted them was momentarily gone, replaced by the need for connection. Every touch, every kiss, was like a silent promise that, whatever awaited them, they would face it together.

The passion that surged between them was powerful and untamed, as if they were finally finding a way to release the tension of the past days and lose themselves in each other. Their hands trembled as they explored one another, discovering each place that had remained hidden until now. Their eyes were filled with passion and anticipation, as if they wanted to capture each second and store it deep within their memory.

Myrto's breath was uneven, and every movement filled Aris with a sense of completeness he had never known. Her touch was tender, full of devotion, while her lips sought his, leaving whispered words of love and desire. Aris, in turn, wanted nothing more than to feel her closer, as if their souls could merge into something that would give them strength for whatever lay ahead.

A Moment Just for Them

This moment was theirs alone, detached from the world and the troubles that circled them. The room was filled with the intensity of their presence, each touch and kiss binding them closer together. Their breaths fell into sync, and their passion flowed like a current they could neither stifle nor control. Every movement was a silent promise, sealing the mutual love and devotion that held them together.

It was as though they were trying to escape the shadow of Karras and the threat that loomed over them, creating a world of their own—protected and safe. Aris felt a deep need to protect her, to keep her away from all the dangers that surrounded them.

The night moved slowly, and they both lost themselves in each other. Time seemed to have stopped, and the sound of their hearts filled the space. Every whisper, every touch, drew them closer, as though they were creating a memory that would stay with them forever—writing a story of love and trust that no one could take from them.

Later, as the first rays of the sun broke through, the two remained entwined, their hands clasped tightly. Myrto had fallen asleep in his arms, and Aris watched her, lost in thought. For the first time, he felt he had something worth fighting for with all his strength.

That morning, their embrace felt like the only safe place in the world.

Back to Reality

The next morning, reality returned with all its weight. As the sun rose, Aris and Myrto, still enveloped in the warmth of the moment they had shared, understood they couldn't linger in this fleeting peace. Karras was still out there, and his looming threat weighed heavily upon them. They knew they couldn't afford to simply hide or rely solely on the evidence they'd gathered. They needed help—someone who truly understood the depth of the danger and the power of the truth.

They decided to reach out to Stelios, a seasoned journalist with a long history of exposing scandals and bringing buried truths to light. He was someone who knew Karras, his reputation, and the extent of his networks—someone who could not only reveal Karras's secrets but also provide them with protection from the lurking threats.

The Meeting with Stelios

The meeting was set up at a secluded café, away from prying eyes and ears. Stelios sat at the back, at a table near the wall that offered a clear view of the entrance—a subtle display of his cautious nature and years of investigative experience. When he saw Aris and Myrto enter, he gestured for them to approach, his gaze sharp and serious.

Aris and Myrto took their seats across from him, and Stelios observed them intently, as if assessing their sincerity in deciding to take on this case. "I've heard rumors about the two of you and your plans," he said, his eyes never wavering. "You should know that what you're trying to expose will have serious repercussions. Karras has people everywhere, and his power reaches far further than you might realize."

Aris took a deep breath, knowing this conversation wouldn't be easy. "We understand, Stelios. But we have all the evidence. Daphne gathered it at the risk of her life, and we can't let Karras go unpunished."

Stelios nodded, a glimmer of understanding flickering in his expression. "I get it. Daphne was a good journalist. She knew how to uncover the truth, but she also understood the risks." His voice held a note of sadness, as if remembering her fight.

Stelios leaned in, making the tone of the conversation even more serious and direct. "If we move forward with this publication, you need to realize the pressure you'll face. Karras isn't the type to simply let anyone tarnish his name or dismantle his organization. You two are now targets, and there's no turning back."

Myrto glanced at Aris, her eyes reflecting her determination. "We're ready," she replied firmly. "This truth needs to come to light, no matter the risks."

Stelios remained silent for a moment, as if weighing their resolve. Finally, he nodded. "Alright, then. I'll help you. But we must be extremely careful. We'll create a safety net around both the information and you two. If danger arises, you must disappear until I can orchestrate the release in a way that protects you and preserves the investigation."

Aris felt a sense of relief, as if they had gained a powerful ally in their fight. He knew Stelios wasn't just any journalist—he was a man who understood the shadowy corridors of power and the dangers lurking within.

The Preparation

The three of them began meticulously planning their next steps together, examining every detail of the evidence they had gathered. Stelios gave them clear instructions on how to safeguard and handle their sensitive information. "This investigation won't be released in one go," he explained. "We'll publish it in stages, piece by piece, so it remains in the public eye continuously. Each time they try to bury it, it will come back stronger."

Aris and Myrto listened intently, realizing they were now part of something much bigger than they'd ever imagined. Stelios went on, explaining how they would need to organize their files, create secure backups, and make the publication irreversible and impossible to dismantle.

"You'll need to keep a low profile and avoid drawing unnecessary attention until we're fully prepared," Stelios cautioned. "Karras will be looking for every possible way to track you down. If he suspects you're working with me, he'll stop at nothing to stop us."

Aris nodded, grasping the full gravity of the situation. Myrto, her expression resolute, squeezed Aris's hand under the table—a silent promise that they would face whatever came their way, together.

They knew the risks they were taking, but they were determined to break the silence.

Shadows of the Past

Stelios delved into the documents that Aris and Myrto had handed him. The breadth of evidence was both impressive and alarming—documents, transaction records, lists of names, and encrypted communications revealing just how deeply Karras's organization had infiltrated circles of power. As he carefully examined each detail, he began to grasp the complexity of the network that supported Karras's operations.

While taking notes in a notebook beside him, his gaze fell on a small silver object that Aris had casually placed on the table. It was the silver tag that Aris had found next to Daphne's open box. Without immediately commenting, Stelios picked it up and examined it with curiosity.

The tag was small and worn, suggesting that it had changed hands many times or seen frequent use. One side had a half-erased letter, which appeared to be an "L," though its edge was worn enough to leave open the possibility that it was another letter or even a symbol. Stelios held it up to the light, trying to discern the mark more clearly.

"What's this?" he asked, casting a sharp, probing look at Aris and Myrto.

Aris met his gaze and explained, "I found it next to Daphne's box at her house. It was open when we last saw it. I don't know who it belongs to or if I've ever seen anything like it before."

Stelios examined the tag again, thoughtfully. The unclear letter might signal the identity of someone close to Daphne, or perhaps even someone connected to Karras's network. Still, he hesitated to jump to conclusions; the half-erased mark could lead them to a vital person—or steer them in the wrong direction.

"We'll need to look at this closely," Stelios said, setting the tag aside before continuing with his analysis of the documents. "We can't be certain what this letter means. It could be an 'L,' maybe half an 'M,' or perhaps it means nothing at all. But every small detail might just lead us somewhere important."

The Publication of the Evidence

Stelios began releasing the incriminating evidence with calculated precision, gradually building tension around the impending scandal. Each article was like a small bomb detonating in the public eye, exposing parts of the corrupt network Karras had woven and unveiling connections with politicians and business figures who had supported his illegal empire.

The initial publications were subtle, hinting at the existence of a criminal organization pulling strings behind major scandals and illicit financial transactions. However, the evidence soon became more explicit, with details proving the involvement of high-profile public figures. The public began to feel the impact and took a keen interest, while many with ties to the truth worried that their names might soon appear in print.

Aris followed Stelios's publications with mixed emotions. On one hand, he felt a sense of satisfaction seeing the truth finally come to light and public awareness growing. On the other, a lingering sense of caution gripped him. He couldn't shake off his thoughts about the silver tag with the faint letter he had been trying to interpret for some time. The initial "L" haunted him, but the idea that it might actually be an "M" kept nagging at him.

Could that faint "M" be connected to Myrto? It was a thought that disturbed him, and every time he tried to push it away, it crept back, leaving him with an underlying fear. Myrto was always by his side, loyal and determined to support him. However, her past association with Karras and her knowledge of intricate details about the case continued to unsettle him.

Aris didn't want to believe that the woman with whom he had shared so much could be betraying him. Yet, his mind couldn't let go of the possibility, and the fear of betrayal kept him on guard. He resolved to stay discreet and decided not to mention his doubts to Myrto. He hoped that by closely watching her reactions to the upcoming publications, he might discern whether his fears were justified or if he was merely falling victim to his own suspicions.

As the publications continued, Aris scrutinized Myrto's every move, every word, searching for any hint that might reveal her true intentions. Though the weight of his suspicions lay heavily on him, it also fueled his determination to push forward, knowing that Karras's network would soon unravel.

Meanwhile, Karras watched helplessly as his empire was systematically dismantled in the public eye. Each revelation was like a knife cutting into the reputation and influence he had painstakingly built over the years. Unable to bear the sight of his life's work crumbling on the front pages, he felt a wave of fury and fear—a recognition that the consequences could be devastating for him and his associates if the revelations continued.

Desperate to reclaim control, Karras ordered his most trusted men to track Aris and Myrto around the clock. He knew that these two were his link to Stelios and the source of the leaks. His plan was simple yet ruthless: find a way to silence Aris and Myrto and, in the process, eliminate any evidence against him.

Realizing that Stelios was too well-protected to be an easy target, Karras turned his full focus to Aris and Myrto, seeing them as the weaker link. He believed that if he could capture and manipulate them to hand over the code and documents, he could halt the damning disclosures and erase every piece of incriminating evidence.

Time was no longer on his side, and Karras knew it. Each new article brought him closer to ruin, leaving him with no choice but to take matters into his own hands. With cold calculation, he devised a trap—a complex web from which Aris and Myrto would have no escape. He would lure them into a dead-end, a point of no return, where they would be forced to face the full extent of his wrath.

The clock was ticking, and Karras was prepared to use every tool, every ally, and every ounce of cunning he had to pull Aris and Myrto into his trap. His only goal now was to end their interference for good, extinguishing the threat they posed to his empire once and for all.

The Turning Point

Karras's eyes narrowed, a flicker of anger crossing his cold expression. He was not accustomed to defiance, and Aris's resolve only strengthened his determination to break them. With a motion of his hand, Karras signaled for his men to close in, each one strategically positioned to prevent any escape. The tension thickened in the air as the standoff began, and the small crowd of onlookers in the café grew silent, unaware of the gravity of what was unfolding.

Myrto felt a surge of fear but remained composed, sensing Aris's unyielding resolve beside her. She could see the same look of steely determination in his eyes—the one that had guided them through every obstacle. Yet now, faced with the ruthless Karras and his mercenaries, the stakes had never been higher.

"Enough games," Karras growled, his tone darkening. "You've had your fun. But now, you're going to tell me everything, and you're going to do it now." He leaned closer, his voice dropping to a chilling whisper. "Or I promise you, this will be your final act."

Aris took a deep breath, steadying himself, and held his ground. "We've come too far to back down now," he replied, his voice unwavering. "If you think threats are enough to make us betray the truth, then you've underestimated us."

Karras's jaw clenched. For the first time, he realized that perhaps his usual methods might not work on these two. He had counted on fear, on desperation, but they were clearly fueled by something much stronger—a commitment to justice, perhaps, or maybe even something deeper that he couldn't fully grasp. Whatever it was, he would have to break it piece by piece.

"Then let's see how long that resolve lasts," Karras hissed, motioning for his men to tighten the circle around them.

First, Karras commanded his men to track every movement of Aris and Myrto, to learn their meeting places, their potential allies, and the locations where they felt safest. For days, Karras's men discreetly followed them, noting every step they took—from their daily routines to their most secretive meetings. They were determined to find the perfect moment to strike. Karras didn't just want to eliminate them; he wanted to crush them psychologically, to make them feel the betrayal and entrapment he had meticulously planned.

The right opportunity soon presented itself. Karras learned that Aris and Myrto had arranged a meeting with Stelios at a secluded café in the suburbs, far from prying eyes. The choice of an isolated spot was ideal for Karras, who saw it as the perfect chance to strike without distractions. He knew that if he ambushed them there, they would feel completely cornered, with no option but to surrender.

Immediately, he ordered his men to position themselves around the café and along the route leading to it, ready to act on his command. The instructions were clear: allow no chance for escape. Karras wanted to ensure that Aris and Myrto would fall into his trap without any possibility of resistance.

On the day of the meeting, Karras waited patiently at the spot he had chosen to ensnare them. Sitting at the back of the café, he had a clear view of the entrance, covering every angle. He watched with cold confidence as his targets approached. Myrto and Aris entered the café, unaware of Karras's presence or of his men surrounding them.

When they finally left the café, Karras's men swiftly and silently surrounded them, and Karras himself stepped forward with his familiar, icy demeanor. "Did you really think you could escape so easily?" he sneered, his voice dripping with mockery. His gaze was hard and unyielding, signaling that the final confrontation had arrived..

Aris and Myrto immediately grasped the gravity of the situation. They were trapped, and any chance of escape was out of the question. Karras advanced slowly, deliberately, as his men closed in, ensuring that no route was left open. "Now," Karras declared, his voice as cold as steel, "you're going to give me everything you know—the code, the documents... everything. This is your last chance."

Despite the tension in the air, Aris stood his ground, unflinching. His eyes moved briefly to Myrto before settling on Karras, filled with unbreakable resolve. "You're not getting anything," he replied, his stance a silent promise that he would resist to the very end.

Karras, seething with rage, motioned to his men, who stepped closer, their movements sharp and menacing. "Don't make the mistake of thinking you have options, Aris," he said, his voice icy with anger. "My organization is far more powerful than you can imagine. You're nothing but a small obstacle, one that will be crushed if you don't back down."

Myrto glanced at Aris, her gaze filled with both worry and silent support. She knew they were trapped, but her presence beside him strengthened Aris, who decided it was time to play his last card.

"The evidence you're after... it's already in safe hands," Aris replied. Karras's expression darkened, realizing that his carefully laid trap might not yield the results he'd hoped for.

With a sarcastic smile, Karras looked between Aris and Myrto, letting out a deep sigh, as if preparing to reveal a truth that he knew would shake them. He turned his gaze to Myrto, eyes full of contempt, before shifting his focus back to Aris.

"I have a story to tell you, Aris," he began, his tone dripping with cold irony. "A story you might not know... or perhaps one you refused to believe."

Aris stared back, uncertain, a growing unease building within him. Karras continued, addressing them both.

“You see, Myrto didn't just happen to come into your life by chance,” he said confidently. “When I realized you could become a threat, I needed a way to keep tabs on you. That's when I decided to use Myrto. She was my most loyal ally—and something more.”

A chill ran down Aris's spine. Karras's words seemed unbelievable, but the way Myrto avoided his gaze made him begin to wonder.

Karras continued with cold determination, a mocking smile on his face. "Myrto was my lover, Aris. She was my right hand, the one person I trusted more than anyone. She was the best at seduction, at getting close, at gaining people's trust. I instructed her to approach you, to become your shadow, to offer you her love—or at least the illusion of it—so that I could learn everything I needed about you."

Aris felt the ground slip out from under his feet. Scenes from their moments together flashed through his mind—each touch, each look now seemed like part of an elaborate deception. He didn't want to believe what he was hearing, but Myrto's refusal to meet his gaze only deepened his doubts.

"Does the café where you first met ring any bells?" Karras continued, his voice dripping with scorn. "It was all staged from the beginning. I arranged for you to be there; I knew how to place her by your side, how to trap you. And Myrto? She played her part to perfection. She gave you exactly what you needed—a partner, a confidant, someone you could trust."

Myrto, head bowed, seemed to be struggling with her emotions. It was clear that there was truth in Karras's words, but she had yet to explain why she had stayed by Aris's side.

"You were just a pawn to us," Karras added, his tone brimming with arrogance. "Every time she sent me information, every move you made—I knew it all. And then... something changed."

Myrto raised her gaze, tears glistening in her eyes. "I stopped playing the role you gave me, Karras," she said, her voice trembling. "What began as a plan to control him became something I couldn't control. My trust and connection with Aris were real. I'm not yours anymore."

Karras looked at her, momentarily thrown off by her defiance. "What did you say?" he spat, his face contorted with rage. "Your loyalty! You've always been part of my plan. You're nothing but a traitor and a coward, like all the weak people who forget their true purpose."

Aris, shaken and feeling betrayed, felt a wave of pain overwhelm him. He lifted his head to look at Myrto, his eyes filled with disappointment, trying to grasp if there had ever been anything genuine in what they had shared.

As the weight of betrayal settled heavily in his heart, Aris's mind flashed back to the silver tag he had found in Daphne's house. At the time, the faint letter engraved on it had seemed like a vague clue, perhaps just a coincidence. But now, everything fell into place.

With a barely audible whisper, he murmured, "It was the letter M..." His eyes widened as the pieces began to fall into place in his mind. The tag wasn't a sign from some unknown associate—it belonged to Myrto. She had been the one who broke into Daphne's box, thinking it held the code Karras sought.

He turned to Myrto, his gaze sharper than ever, filled with questions and accusations. "You broke into Daphne's box," he said, his voice heavy with disappointment. "You were searching for the code... for Karras."

Keeping his eyes fixed on Myrto, Aris allowed the pain and disillusionment to flood his thoughts. His mind wandered back, recalling every detail, each small clue that now seemed like undeniable proof of her betrayal.

"How could you, Myrto?" he thought, his voice trembling with suppressed anger. "All those signs... I saw them, but I refused to believe."

He remembered their first meeting in that café, how she had approached him with a natural ease that had captivated him. "Was that kindness and understanding real, or were you just playing your role? All those little moments I thought we shared... were they part of your plan too?"

He continued to recall the times she had shown him loyalty and tenderness, standing by him through the roughest moments of their investigation. "You were there to support me, sharing my fears, and I trusted you. You were by my side when I had no one else to lean on. You were there when I felt the weight of this case pressing down on me, too heavy to carry alone."

And yet... you were planted there, watching, ready to betray me."

Aris's thoughts returned to the moments he had confided in her about Daphne, about her significance, and about the box that held her secrets. "You knew how important that box was to me. You knew there was something precious hidden inside it. You were the only one who knew about the code and the painful lengths I was going to in order to uncover the truth. And still, you didn't hesitate. When you saw the chance, you broke into her box, searching for the code that would give you access to everything Karras wanted."

The thought made him clench his jaw in anger. "And I, the fool, let you into my life, let you become my anchor. I lost myself, believing I'd found someone I could trust completely. But you were playing a role—you were placed beside me to lead me to this very moment, to fall into the trap Karras had so carefully laid out. You were here to extract the code, to get close to me, to control me..."

He felt the weight of disappointment seeping into every thought. All the details, every whisper of doubt he'd ignored, now stood before him as undeniable evidence of her betrayal. "I was so blind. I didn't want to see what was right in front of me. I saw a woman who loved me, but you were something else entirely... You were Karras's woman, his instrument, the betrayal I never saw coming. You were his lover and his right hand. And I believed in you... I made you a part of my life, while you sought every opportunity to use me."

Aris felt a deep pain, as if each word he thought cut through him, every memory becoming a thorn piercing deeper into his heart. "You were the one I should have kept away from. You were the one who stole my peace, who made me believe in a love that never existed. How could you?"

Aris's mind spiraled into pain and betrayal, every memory of Myrto now feeling like a carefully crafted lie. Every kiss, every word, and every night they had shared now tormented him. He had handed over his heart, his trust, and she had deceived him with such ease.

"When I looked into your eyes, I thought I saw honesty. I thought you were different. But it was all an illusion, a well-rehearsed act. Even in our most tender moments, your purpose wasn't to stay by my side—it was to destroy me. You were Karras's agent. From our first meeting, all you wanted was to get close to me, to win my trust, and in the end, take away the one thing I held dearest."

Aris felt his anger intensify as the pieces of betrayal fell into place in his mind. "And the box... Daphne's box, where everything sacred left of her was hidden. How could you, Myrto? How could you desecrate something so precious to me just to complete Karras's scheme? Was it just another step in your play of betrayal? Were you looking for the code and assumed it was hidden there? What did you think you'd find?"

Disappointment and rage consumed him, his face tightening with fury. "And me? I fell right into your trap. I trusted you, opened every door for you, shared every secret. I told you about Daphne, about the code, about everything that haunted me, and you were nothing but Karras's tool to destroy me. You were here to deceive me. You were the last person I expected to betray me, yet..."

Aris's voice cracked, dropping to a pained whisper, as if even saying it aloud was an admission he could barely bring himself to make. "I believed in you, Myrto. I did everything to trust you. I let you into my life... And now I see that you were just the darkest betrayal."

As his words left his lips, Myrto looked at him in agony, knowing that her truth needed to come to light. She took a step forward, trying to reach him, to make him listen, to understand.

With tears in her eyes, Myrto looked at him desperately, stretching her hand toward him, hoping to explain. She knew that every word she spoke now had to be genuine, for Aris's trust had already shattered, and only an honest confession might make a difference.

"Aris, please, listen to me..." she said, her voice trembling. "Yes, it's true that Karras sent me. I was close to him once. I thought he was my only way forward, my escape from a life full of danger and dependency. When he made me approach you, at first, I saw it as just a job. But..." She paused, taking a deep breath as tears streamed down her cheeks.

"But things changed, Aris. The more I got to know you, the more time I spent with you, something inside me shifted. I no longer wanted to be Karras's tool. I wanted to stay by your side... genuinely. Whatever I had with him was nothing but a lie. It was all an act. The only real thing in my life... is you."

Aris looked at her, still wary, struggling to believe her words. But Myrto didn't stop.

"I never touched Daphne's box," she continued, her voice filled with fervor and sincerity. "The code never mattered to me from the moment I decided to leave Karras behind. When I met you, I realized I finally had a chance to escape him, to find something real. Please, believe me. Every feeling I have for you is true... even if it started the wrong way."

Her voice broke again, and she lowered her gaze, overwhelmed by despair. "I know I have no right to ask anything of you, Aris. I know my words may not be enough to fix the damage I've done. But please... try to understand that I love you. Every single thing we shared, every moment, was real to me."

Aris stood silently, wrestling with himself, trying to decide whether he could ever believe her confession. The truth lay before him, and his heart needed to choose—could he ever forgive her, or would she forever be the greatest mistake of his life?

As the tension reached its peak, a shadowed figure emerged, breaking the silence and sending a chill through the room. It was Nikos, Aris's childhood friend. He looked different now—colder and more calculated, his gaze filled with darkness and resolve. At the sound of his voice, everyone turned to him, frozen by his sudden appearance.

"Even Karas stared at him in stunned disbelief, with a look of terror painted across his face."

"N... Nikos? It was you? All this time..." Aris whispered, his voice trembling.

Aris, equally stunned, struggled to comprehend this new revelation. The faded initial he had been seeing for so long finally made sense. The "N"... it belonged to Nikos.

Nikos approached slowly, his eyes glinting with a strange mix of sadness and a hardness Aris had never seen before. "It had to be this way, Aris. I had to play my role to the very end. Someone needed to protect Karras, to make sure everything we built wouldn't fall apart. I was the one behind it all... Karras was just the face of the organization."

Aris felt his heart tighten painfully. He couldn't believe that the man he considered a brother, the one with whom he shared every childhood memory, was behind all of this. Every betrayal, every trap... it all pointed to Nikos.

Myrto, witnessing Nikos reveal the truth, felt her own betrayal pale in comparison to what Nikos had done. And yet, Nikos showed no sign of regret.

Standing straight, his gaze heavy, Nikos took a deep breath before beginning his story. His voice was cold, almost detached, as if he were speaking about someone else's life.

"Aris... I was never the person you thought I was," he began, his voice trembling with tension. "From a young age, I searched for a way to escape my fate, to find my place in a world that didn't seem to have a place for me. When I met Karras, he offered me something I'd never had before—power, control. I became his thoughts, the mind behind his every move. He was the face of the organization, but I was the shadow, the one pulling the strings, unseen."

Aris stared at him, stunned, trying to comprehend the depth of the betrayal. Nikos continued, swept away by his memories.

"When I started, I believed I could control everything, that I could use the organization to get whatever I wanted. But over time, the darkness we spread began to consume me. I was trapped, Aris. Everything was arranged in such a way that there was no way out. I was in so deep that I couldn't see any light."

Nikos's voice softened, and sadness clouded his eyes. "Then Daphne came along. She was smarter than we imagined, more cautious. She sensed something was off and started watching me. She began to suspect that someone more dangerous was behind Karras, someone hidden. She started digging through our records, investigating our movements, and each day, she got closer to the truth."

Nikos took a deep breath, his eyes darkening further.

"I had no other choice," Nikos continued, his voice breaking. "I knew that if Daphne uncovered the truth, she wouldn't stop. And I didn't want to hurt her, Aris. For the first time, I felt fear... guilt, something human inside me. I tried to deter her, to push her away, but she wouldn't relent. Every step she took brought her closer to the heart of the organization. So... I had to erase her traces."

His voice cracked, and Aris could see the internal struggle—the weight of guilt Nikos bore for what he'd done.

"I foolishly thought that if Daphne disappeared, I could go on, that everything would settle down. But her loss brought nothing but emptiness. The organization kept demanding more of me, my shadow grew darker, and my guilt became unbearable. So when I learned that you, Aris, had begun investigating... I knew I had reached the end of the road. There was no escape."

Nikos bowed his head, letting his words linger like ghosts in the air. Aris, deeply hurt and shaken, looked at his childhood friend, struggling to understand how someone he'd known his entire life had turned into the monster now standing before him.

The sound of police cars and helicopters drew closer, their lights flashing red and blue in the night. Aris and Myrto exchanged a glance filled with urgent concern and began searching for an escape route.

They broke into a sprint, weaving through the narrow alleyways, with Nikos—his face twisted in hatred and despair—close behind. Gunshots echoed through the space, each step growing heavier with tension. The building was surrounded, the police closing in, and their options for escape were dwindling rapidly.

Suddenly, a gunshot rang out. Myrto shoved Aris behind a metal dumpster just as Karras, standing across from them, took a bullet to the chest. His eyes widened in shock, unable to process the turn of events, and he collapsed to the ground with a heavy thud. In that instant, his empire crumbled, leaving nothing behind but shadows and ashes.

Nikos, now a fugitive himself, realized he was cornered. In a final, desperate attempt, he faced a squad of police officers while Aris and Myrto pursued him from behind. The officers encircled him, their flashlights trained on him, making any chance of escape impossible.

For a fleeting moment, Nikos turned his gaze toward Aris, his eyes filled with a haunting blend of regret and farewell. "I'm sorry, Aris," he whispered, his voice laden with guilt and sorrow. "I wasn't strong enough to escape the darkness."

Before Aris could react, Nikos raised his weapon and, with a swift motion, pulled the trigger, ending his own life. The shot reverberated through the frozen silence, and Nikos's body fell lifeless to the ground.

Aris and Myrto stood still, absorbing the magnitude of the tragedy that had just unfolded before them. Betrayal, loss, and the heavy price they had all paid left a profound ache—one that would be nearly impossible to overcome.

Suddenly, a group of police officers called out for them to stop, their flashlights illuminating the scene. Myrto and Aris exchanged a tense glance, and Aris slowly raised his hands to show they meant no harm. They knew the moment of truth had arrived—they would have to explain everything that had happened.

"We're the ones who helped expose the truth about Karras and his organization," Aris said, trying to steady his voice. "Nikos... my friend... he was the mastermind behind it all. He paid the price... as did Karras."

The police, recognizing the gravity of the case and listening to Aris's words, grasped the weight of the revelations that had just surfaced. The chief, with an expression that conveyed both understanding and concern, approached Aris and Myrto, asking them to accompany him to the station. There, they would have the opportunity to provide the necessary explanations and fully unravel the dark and complex truth behind the case.

After giving detailed accounts to the authorities, Aris and Myrto were led out of the police building. The first light of dawn began to spread across the sky, offering a sense of relief after a seemingly endless night of betrayal and loss. The sunrise brought the promise of a new beginning, but Aris still felt the heavy burden of Nikos's betrayal following him.

They stood quietly for a moment, gazing at the horizon. They knew this chapter would stay with them forever. The truth had emerged, but the cost had been heavy, and the wounds it left would need time to heal. Myrto took his hand and whispered, "It's over, Aris... we can make a new beginning."

The Fall of the Organization

After the deaths of Karras and Nikos, the evidence collected by Aris, Myrto, and Stelios began to make headlines in a way that could no longer be ignored. Every file, document, and recorded conversation revealed the vast scale and reach of the organization—not just within their own country, but extending internationally, touching powerful figures and financial powerhouses. The organization that Nikos and Karras had built had infiltrated various sectors—politics, commerce, banking—creating a web of corruption that seemed to reach everywhere.

Scandals broke at an astonishing rate. International media outlets picked up the story, recognizing that this wasn't just a local issue, but a global scandal with profound implications on political decisions and economic activities worldwide. Each new revelation struck like a bombshell, forcing authorities to act swiftly, with no opportunity for cover-ups. Police and prosecutors began arresting top members of the organization, both domestically and abroad.

It soon became clear that the network Nikos had built with Karras's help was involved in illegal financing, money laundering, and even influence peddling at high political levels. The exposure had a massive impact—not just in their country, but also on the international circles tied to the organization's interests. Many powerful individuals who once believed themselves above the law were now exposed and forced to answer for their actions.

Every page of Daphne's files confirmed what she had always suspected: the organization wasn't just a local pocket of corruption; it was a global machine that controlled and influenced lives, making decisions driven solely by profit and power, with no moral boundaries. Daphne had realized early on the magnitude of what she had uncovered and had resolved to press forward, no matter the cost. Every move she made was dangerous, and she knew that her investigation could cost her everything—and in the end, it did.

Yet, her determination not to give up was vindicated. Daphne left behind a code of honor—a legacy proving that the courage of one person could shake even the darkest networks of power. Her memory became a symbol of justice for those who had suffered from the organization's actions, inspiring others who wished to fight for the truth.

As Aris watched events unfold, he felt a sense of closure. Daphne's sacrifice had not been in vain—her fight lived on through those she trusted and the friends who remained loyal to the end. The organization had collapsed, and the roots of corruption were exposed to the world. Justice had been served, and Daphne had been vindicated.

The code "Forever" became a symbol of hope and integrity, reminding everyone that the fight for truth never ends. Just as Daphne had never stopped battling for justice, "Forever" marked her eternal legacy—a call to all who would dare to face the darkness.

Aris stood on the edge of a cliff overlooking the beach where he and Daphne had spent their first night together—the same beach where they had discovered the first clue to the code. The horizon began to glow with the first light of dawn, casting a serene glow over the sea. Yet inside, he felt the turmoil of the storm he had endured—the journey that had brought him here, every painful moment along the way. In his hands, he held the silver tag—a small artifact tied to everything that had happened: the darkness, the betrayal, but also the hard-won truth he had uncovered.

He turned to look at Myrto, who stood silently beside him, her eyes reflecting both sorrow and relief. They had faced countless trials together, and in the end, she had chosen to stand by him, even when the cost was immense. What had begun as a betrayal had transformed into an unexpected partnership—a bond forged in the shadows, shaped by hardship and sacrifice.

Aris stepped closer, holding out the tag to her. It was now engraved with the word "FOREVER." “This belongs to you now,” he said, his voice steady. “A symbol of everything we’ve been through—of your choice to stay by my side, and of our decision to build something new from the ashes.”

Myrto looked at him, her expression softening with warmth. “I’ll never stop fighting for the truth, Aris. No matter what’s happened, I’m here—with you.”

Aris pulled her into a tight embrace, feeling, for the first time in what felt like ages, the weight of loss and pain beginning to lift. Together, they had uncovered the truth, dismantled a ruthless organization, and honored Daphne’s memory.

“Forever,” Aris whispered, letting the word escape on his breath—a word that had guided them both to this moment. The silver tag glinted in the dawn light, as if it carried with it the promise of rebirth, devotion, and Daphne's eternal memory.

With newfound determination, they turned their backs on the past, leaving behind the shadows, ready to move forward together into the light—building their own story. A story that would continue to fight for justice, for truth, and for those who never stopped seeking what was right.

The End

About the Author

With a passion for mysteries and crime stories, the author dives into the depths of human psychology and the intricate journey of uncovering the truth. Fascinated by the delicate balance between ethics and justice, each story follows the relentless pursuit of righteousness, where every clue, every choice, holds significant weight. The author's love for unraveling enigmas and tackling complex criminal challenges weaves a gripping narrative, inviting readers into a world where light constantly battles the shadows. Drawing on a background in [related field or experience, if desired], the author crafts stories that unfold like puzzles, celebrating the transformative power of discovery.

This work is dedicated to readers who love suspense, mystery-solving, and the unwavering pursuit of justice.

Don't miss out!

Visit the website below and you can sign up to receive emails whenever ATHANASIOS VOULGARIS publishes a new book. There's no charge and no obligation.

https://books2read.com/r/B-A-BWVQC-BVCHF

Also by ATHANASIOS VOULGARIS

The Miracle of Friendship Christmas in the Forest
CODE ForeveR

www.ingramcontent.com/pod-product-compliance
Lightning Source LLC
LaVergne TN
LVHW040946150826
845672LV00002B/568

* 9 7 9 8 2 3 0 0 3 6 5 6 2 *